CASEY AND
THE GREAT IDEA

Mark F. Casagrande
P. O. Box 695
Alpine, N. J. 07620

**Other APPLE PAPERBACKS
You Will Want to Read:**

CASEY AND THE GREAT IDEA

By
JOAN LOWERY NIXON

Illustrated by
Amy Rowen

AN
APPLE
PAPERBACK

SCHOLASTIC BOOK SERVICES
New York Toronto London Auckland Sydney Tokyo

ISBN-0-590-40618-3

Text copyright © 1980 by Joan Lowery Nixon. Illustrations copyright © 1980 by Amy Rowen. All rights reserved. This edition is published by Scholastic Inc., 730 Broadway, New York, NY 10003, by arrangement with E.P. Dutton, Inc. APPLE PAPERBACKS is a registered trademark of Scholastic Inc.

12 11 10 9 8 7 6 5 4 3 2 1   5 6 7 8 9/8   0/9

With love to Eileen,
who has a few great ideas
of her own

1 | The First Step Toward Trouble

"Be reasonable, Casey," Mr. Robinson said. "We have always had separate physical education programs for boys and girls at this school." He peered at her from under his furry, gray eyebrows, looking like a squirrel which was ready to scamper up a tree if she made a sudden move.

Casey wished she were like her Aunt Eugenia—cool, poised, and in complete control in her fight for equal rights for women. But unfortunately, Casey was only twelve and had a tendency to turn pink when she got upset, and trip over her feet, and blurt out the wrong things at the wrong times.

But she was determined. She pushed back a strand of unruly red hair that had strayed into the corner of her mouth, and leaned on the principal's desk. "Please think about it, Mr. Robinson!" she said. She waved her arms in an imploring gesture that sent his gleaming, wooden nameplate soaring into the wastepaper basket.

Mr. Robinson looked pained. "I don't think we need to talk about this any longer, Casey." He accepted the nameplate, which she had fished out of the wastepaper basket, and put it back on his desk as firmly as though he were nailing it there. He added, "We could talk, instead, about this disruptive behavior you've been exhibiting lately. It seems as though you are being influenced by your aunt. Eugenia Gladheart is your aunt, isn't she?"

"Yes, she is," Casey said. She tilted her chin a little higher.

"I've read about her women's rights activities."

"She's president of the Beverly Glen group," Casey interrupted.

He leaned toward her, and his eyes glittered as he spaced out the words. "And I saw her on television as she was being taken to jail!"

"That's not fair," Casey said. "She had gone to interview the head of an auto parts company, to ask him if the women in his employ were being paid fairly. And he grinned at her and told her she had great legs, so she dumped the papers in his out basket on his head."

"That's assault," Mr. Robinson said.

2

"The charges were dropped," Casey said. "The man's wife made him drop them." She stood as tall as she could and looked at him over the tip of her nose. "I'm sorry you won't listen to reason about integrating the boys' and girls' sports programs, but I want you to know, this was my own idea. Eugenia had nothing to do with it."

Casey stalked out of Mr. Robinson's office before he had a chance to answer, closing the door firmly.

Alison, who was waiting in the hallway for her, took one look at her friend's face and said, "Oh-oh! You didn't get into trouble, did you?"

"No. Mr. Robinson just wouldn't listen to reason," Casey said. "He's a very stubborn man. He also doesn't like my Aunt Eugenia."

"He would if he knew her," Alison said. She tried to match her stride to Casey's as they left the building and started the walk toward their homes. "Eugenia is so beautiful, with that dark, dark hair and blue eyes and . . ."

Casey interrupted. "Don't call Eugenia beautiful. She doesn't like it."

"If it was me, I would," Alison said. "I'd like to be beautiful enough for Randolph Mantooth to notice me."

Casey shrugged. "How is Randolph Mantooth going to notice you? He's a television star, and you never go anyplace where you could meet television stars."

Alison nodded confidently. "Someday I might, and I'm getting ready. Every day I do that exercise with soup cans to get bigger on top, and I eat eggs to make my hair curly, and I think positive. Rosalie Mertz told me that would help."

"Who's Rosalie Mertz?" Casey asked.

"One of my neighbors," Alison said. "She's a real neat person, Casey. Someday you'll have to meet her."

Casey nodded toward the building they were passing. "Let's stop in at the Quick Shop and get some chocolate bars. We can say hello to Sylvia."

"Okay," Alison said. The two girls crossed the parking lot to the tiny neighborhood self-service store and went inside, Casey, as usual, stumbling over the doorstep.

Sylvia was behind the checkout counter. She looked up quickly through the curtain of her bleached yellow bangs, then relaxed against the back of the metal stool.

"Hey, it's you two," Sylvia said, smiling crookedly.

"I bet working in a store is an interesting career," Casey said, reaching for a chocolate bar.

"Career?" Sylvia laughed. "You call sitting behind this counter day after day a career? Ha! Some career!"

"Well, I mean," Casey said, "you aren't tied to a house, and you're out in the business world, and . . ." Her voice faltered.

Sylvia reached over and patted Casey's hand, choc-

5

olate bar and all. "Honey, believe me, this is not what I consider my career. It's a way of . . . well . . . let's say it's a way of staying alive for now."

"At least you've got lots of good things to eat around here," Alison offered.

"And you don't have to stay in this job if you don't like it," Casey said. "You've got other opportunities."

"My opportunities for the moment are somewhat limited." Sylvia shook her head. "Listen, kids, don't be like me. Stay in school and learn something. Then you can do something. Me, I dropped out in high school, and that's no good."

"But you could go back to school," Casey said. "Or you could study for a General Educational Development test. If you pass, you could get your diploma and go on to college."

"Forget it," Sylvia said. "There's no way I could afford to go back."

Another customer came through the doorway, calling shrilly, "Have you got tapioca pudding? Everybody seems to be out of tapioca pudding!"

Casey and Alison put their money on the counter, and left Sylvia trying to convince the woman that it wasn't a government plot that all the stores were out of tapioca pudding.

"I wouldn't want to work there either," Alison said, munching on her chocolate bar.

"What do you want to do when you're grown-up?" Casey asked. "Do you know yet?" She ate her chocolate in three bites and licked her fingers.

"Sure, I know," Alison said. "I want to marry Randolph Mantooth."

"I mean seriously," Casey said.

"I am serious."

Casey nudged her friend and laughed. "You're always kidding, Alison. Race you to my house!"

"What makes you think I'm kidding?" Alison yelled and ran after Casey.

They were both out of breath as they squeezed past each other to get inside the front door first. They leaned against the wall, giggling until they were breathing normally.

"Where's your mother?" Alison asked. She sniffed the air expectantly, then shrugged. "I hoped she was making cookies again."

"Listen," Casey said. She held a finger to her lips.

From the den came the hesitant, uneven click of typewriter keys.

"She's learning to type," Casey said. "My Aunt Eugenia enrolled her in a typing class for her birthday present. Eugenia and I are going to help Mother learn to fulfill herself."

"Let's go back and say hello," Alison said.

They walked down the inner hallway to the den and

paused at the open door. "Okay if we come in?" Casey asked.

Her mother's smiling face shone under a mop of curly hair that was as red as Casey's. "Please do!" she said. "I'm finished with this list, and I'm so glad! I've been typing for so long, my fingers ache!"

"We could hear you typing, Mom," Casey said as her mother got out of the chair and hugged her. "I think you're improving. It sounded faster."

"I think I've gone from five words a minute to six words a minute, not counting the errors," she said. "But I promised Eugenia I'd type this list for her."

"What list?" Casey asked.

"It's a list of presidents of local companies that seem to be discriminating against women. Eugenia is going to get it copied and sent to all the newspapers and television and radio news departments in Los Angeles."

"It's nice about your learning to type, but I was sort of hoping you'd be making cookies," Alison said. "You make such wonderful cookies."

Mrs. Cooper put an arm around Alison's shoulders and gave her a hug, too. "I just happen to have some butterscotch-nut cookies in the cookie jar," she said. "I'll get a plate of cookies and some glasses of milk, and come back and we'll all have a party."

"It's called a break," Casey said. "When you work in an office, Mom, you can't say, 'We'll take a few minutes and have a party.'"

"Right," Mrs. Cooper said. She sighed and left the room.

"I don't think your mother really likes learning to type," Alison said.

But Casey was staring at the paper her mother had taken from the typewriter. "Hey, Alison! You know who belongs on this list? That male chauvinist, Mr. Robinson!" She rolled the paper back into the typewriter, lining up the margins.

"Casey, you aren't going to put his name on that list!" Alison said.

"Why should it list just adult women who are discriminated against?" Casey asked. "I think women our age count too!"

"Well, sure," Alison said, "but . . ."

With two fingers Casey typed the name carefully and pulled the sheet out of the typewriter. "Maybe someone in the board of education will see Mr. Robinson's name and say, 'Mr. Robinson, for your old-fashioned stand against integrated physical education programs in your school, you're in a lot of trouble!' "

Alison shook her head and said, "Oh, Casey, I don't think Mr. Robinson's the one who'll get into trouble!"

2 | Two Sides to the Story

Alison was right.

The next evening Eugenia came dashing over in such a flurry that little gusts of air seemed to be whirling around her. Right on her heels was a tall, somewhat stoop-shouldered man with a wide smile and eyes that matched his brown hair. For just an instant Casey thought that if Alison should see him, she'd forget all about Randolph Mantooth, but her aunt's next words drove every other thought out of her head.

"Doris! John! Casey!" Eugenia said, throwing her arms out dramatically.

Casey's father and mother got up from their chairs, her father dropping the newspaper from his lap in a heap. Casey, lying on her stomach, wearing her most comfortable jeans and T-shirt, and trying to trace a map of the Suez Canal, sat up and stared.

"I guess that was half of an introduction," Casey's father said. He held out his hand, and the man walked forward and shook it.

"Hi," he said. "I'm Paul Baker."

"How thoughtless of me," Eugenia said with a little sigh. "I just assumed you knew Paul. He did that feature story about my arrest for Channel 12." She smiled up at him, and Casey watched his face soften like butter on hot popcorn.

Mrs. Cooper moved forward. "Come and sit down, Paul . . . Eugenia. For goodness' sakes, don't just stand there. Can I get everyone a cup of coffee? Some butterscotch cookies?"

Eugenia groaned. "Doris, I keep telling you, don't be so domestic."

"But everyone likes coffee and cookies," Mrs. Cooper said in a voice that faded away.

"Right now, we need to talk," Eugenia said. She sat on the sofa, pulling Paul down beside her. "Paul and I have something to tell you."

"Lovely!" Mrs. Cooper's eyes opened wide, and she beamed. She sank into the nearest chair, clasping her hands.

"Oh, Doris!" Eugenia rolled her eyes in exasperation. "What we need to talk about is that list you typed for me. What happened to it?"

"I gave it to you. Don't you remember?"

"I know you gave it to me," Eugenia said. "I'm asking about that last name you added. Why did you add it? Who is he?"

Casey cleared her throat and tried to sound as convincing as she had felt the night before. "I'd better explain that one, Eugenia," she said. "I put that name on your list."

"Why?"

"Because it's the name of our school principal, and I've been trying to get him to integrate the boys' and girls' sports programs, and he won't, so I thought he belonged on your list."

"Oh, Casey!" Eugenia began, but Paul leaned forward.

"Our station was sent a copy of the list, Casey, and I carefully checked the names. That last one puzzled me, so I came to ask Eugenia about it. That's why we're here."

Casey jumped up and went to her aunt. "That was a list of men who are discriminating against women, just because they're female, and the girls in my school are females too, even if we are young."

Eugenia thought a moment. "You have a good point there, Casey. The only problem is that a school isn't like a business. In a school situation, the principal has complete authority."

"You mean it's like a dictatorship?"

13

"Well, no. . . . I mean yes. . . . I mean . . ."
Eugenia shook her head helplessly. "Oh, Casey, I'm afraid we're all in trouble because you put that name on the list."

"Is there any way to keep the list from being published?" Casey's father asked. He rubbed the bald spot on his head the way he did when he was worried.

"I think it's too late for that," Paul answered. "We could probably reach the morning papers, but the story is likely to show up on the late news on a couple of the stations tonight, and some of the radio announcers might have already used it."

"Mr. Robinson might sue us," Eugenia said.

There was a moment of gloomy silence until Casey spoke up. "Could we go to see him and talk to him?" she asked. "Maybe if we explained what happened he'd be understanding and just laugh it off as a big joke."

"Do you really think he'd do that, Casey?" her mother asked.

"No," Casey said.

"I think it's a good idea," Paul said. They all stared at him, but he continued. "Let me call the station and see if I can get a cameraman."

"Camera person," Eugenia said.

"Camera person," Paul repeated. "We could take Casey to Mr. Robinson's house and interview him.

14

That way, he could tell his side of the story, and it might make an interesting short feature for the news tomorrow."

"His side of the story is the unfair side," Casey insisted.

Paul smiled at Eugenia. "It could only give your cause a little extra publicity," he said.

"Casey," Eugenia said firmly, "you should have asked my permission to add that name. I'm all for an integrated sports program. But we've got to do what we can to protect ourselves legally. Do you understand?"

"Of course I understand," Casey said. She sat on the arm of the sofa and stared down at her shoes. "And I'm really sorry if I did everything all wrong."

"I'll make that call now," Paul said. "If I can get a—a camera person, I'll call Mr. Robinson and ask when we can see him."

As soon as Eugenia had led Paul to the kitchen phone, Casey felt her mother's warm hand cover her own, holding it firmly.

Mr. Cooper leaned forward. "After this, when you want to get something accomplished, do something positive, Casey, not something negative."

"Your father is right, Casey," Mrs. Cooper said. "But don't be unhappy. You were trying to do something you believed in."

16

"It looks like I made a king-sized mistake," Casey groaned.

"Everyone makes mistakes," her mother said. "I made the mistake of not reading the list over before I gave it to Eugenia. She made the mistake of not reading it before she had it copied and sent out. We're all in this together."

Casey managed to smile at her parents. "Thanks," she said. "I just hope we don't get sued."

Her mother smiled back and patted Casey's shoulder. "I don't think we will. Mr. Robinson's wife is on the same volunteer shift I'm on in the hospital gift shop, and she's such a friendly person. She's just not the type to have a husband who sues people."

"Oh, Mom! Your thinking is hopeless!" Casey laughed, but at the same time she felt comforted that maybe things were not quite as bad as they seemed.

Eugenia popped back into the room with Paul at her heels. "It's all set," she said. "We'll meet the camera person at Mr. Robinson's house." She turned to Casey. "Mr. Robinson splutters a lot when he talks, doesn't he?"

"Only when he's furious," Casey whispered.

Her mother still kept a firm grip on her hand. "It will take us just a moment to get ready."

"I think it's better if we don't have a whole group descend on him," Paul said. "Suppose you let Casey go with Eugenia and me. We'll take good care of her."

Casey didn't like the twinkle in his eyes, as though this whole thing were an amusing adventure. She pulled her hand away from her mother, embarrassed.

"Okay," she said, getting to her feet.

"Casey," her mother said, "if you're going to be on camera, why don't you change? Surely you don't want to be photographed in those jeans and a T-shirt that says I Am Woman."

"She's fine the way she is," Eugenia said. "Besides, we haven't got time. We'll have to leave right now."

Casey found herself being bustled out the door and into Paul's car. On the way to Mr. Robinson's house she sat between Paul and Eugenia, feeling like the insides of a chicken sandwich as the two of them talked over her head about various approaches to Mr. Robinson. She wondered if anyone besides herself could hear her heart bumping loudly.

In a short time they arrived at the Robinson house. She found herself being introduced to Gladys, a small, round photographer with a short, round Afro, and in a few moments Mr. Robinson was opening his door and scowling at her as though she were a bug in his soup.

A woman with a comfortable coffee-commercial smile slipped up beside her as they moved into the living room and whispered, "You have such a lovely mother, Casey. Please give her my regards."

Casey didn't have time to answer. Mr. Robinson

turned to her and said, "Young lady, you're in more trouble now than any troublemaker could possibly look for!"

Casey gulped. There was no way this situation could turn out right!

3 | Casey Plans a Big Surprise

"Now, Andrew," Mrs. Robinson said. "Give the young lady a chance."

Casey was so interested in watching Gladys adjusting her light bar and swinging her camera onto her shoulder that she missed Paul's conversation with Mr. Robinson. She suddenly realized that the interview was beginning, and Paul was standing close to Mr. Robinson, speaking into a microphone.

Mr. Robinson blinked at the lights and looked out of the corners of his eyes at the camera.

"So we have come to talk to this principal who believes in guiding his students to independence, giving them the spirit to stand up for the ideals they believe in, even when those ideals are not compatible with school policy. Isn't that right, Mr. Robinson?"

"Uh . . . yes. . . . That is . . ." He wobbled between trying to look indignant and trying to look dignified. "Naturally," he managed to say, "we want our students to feel free to express themselves, but as to putting my name on that list . . ."

"With those heads of large corporations and multimillion-dollar businesses," Paul interrupted.

"Yes . . . yes." Mr. Robinson stopped and thought for a moment. "Of course it was irregular, and our sports program is based on guidelines our schools have followed for many years. When our boys get to high school, they'll be competing for college scholarships in sports and . . ."

"Don't many colleges now offer sports scholarships to girls?"

"Oh . . . well, I have heard that more and more are, but the decision about our sports program isn't mine alone, and that is . . ." Mr. Robinson looked wildly back and forth from Paul to the camera.

Paul broke in. "There are two sides to this idea of integrating the boys' and girls' sports programs in the schools. Both sides have their staunch supporters. That freedom to have opposite opinions is what this country is all about, and it's what Mr. Robinson teaches and practices as principal of Lenning Marsh School here in the San Fernando Valley. Congratulations, Mr. Robinson."

Mr. Robinson took the hand Paul was extending and shook it the way he'd shake a dusty rag. "Well . . . thank you. That is, I . . . we do try to teach our students independent thinking, and I suppose in this case . . ." He sighed and stared blankly at the camera.

Paul turned to face the camera. "And so we conclude our interview with Mr. Andrew B. Robinson, one of our outstanding educators of today. This is Paul Baker, Channel 12, Los Angeles."

Gladys turned out the lights, and Paul relaxed, swinging the mike down by his side. "Thank you for a fine interview, Mr. Robinson," he said.

Mrs. Robinson tried to look serious, but a tiny smile kept flickering at the corners of her mouth. "Why, Andrew," she said, "this morning when you woke up, you didn't know you were going to be famous, did you?"

"Famous, or infamous?" he grumbled. He turned to Paul. "I suppose you think all that soft soap got to me!"

Paul remained unruffled. "I think our interview is going to make a good feature for the morning news show," he said.

Mr. Robinson stared at Casey, and she expected him to scowl again. But instead he said, "Casey, I suppose it's a good thing when a young lady has the courage of her convictions, but those convictions shouldn't be expressed in a negative way. There are a lot of positive things you can do to further any cause you might believe in."

"Yes, Mr. Robinson," Casey said. "That's what I was trying to do when I came to see you about the sports program." She grabbed a vase her elbow had bumped and put it back on the end table.

"The s-s-sports program!" Mr. Robinson began to sputter, and Mrs. Robinson quickly ushered them all out of the house.

"It's going to be all right," she said. "Just please, Casey, for goodness' sakes, think about something besides the sports program for a little while!"

After the door shut behind them, Paul said, "Now for some shots of Casey. You don't have to say anything, Casey. I'll just mention the list and how Mr. Robinson's name got on it. You stand next to me."

Casey knew how Mr. Robinson had felt when those lights shone in her face and the camera was aimed at her. She wanted desperately to scratch her chin, but knew she couldn't, and it made her fidget. She was so intent on the photographer, she really didn't pay much attention to what Paul was saying. Finally the ordeal was over, and they were thanking Gladys and piling back into the car.

"That was marvelous, Paul," Eugenia said, looking

up at him. "You handled that situation so tactfully, I'm sure Mr. Robinson won't cause any trouble now."

Paul seemed less sure of himself when he looked at Eugenia. "Uh . . . maybe we could . . . uh . . . get something to drink before I take you home," he suggested.

"No, thanks," Casey said. "I don't drink."

Paul just stared at her as though he had forgotten she was still there, and Eugenia said, "I'd like that, Paul—after we take Casey home."

That was fine with Casey. All she wanted to do was get home, finish the Suez Canal, and phone Alison. Alison would never believe what had happened!

But first, she had to tell her parents every detail, which she surprised herself by remembering, right down to Mrs. Robinson's regards to her mother.

"Now can I use the phone?" she asked.

"She lives on the phone," her father mumbled, but no one told her she couldn't, so she raced to the extension in her parents' bedroom. She climbed with it into the space between the side of the bed and the wall, where she felt snug and secure in her privacy, and dialed the Englemans' unlisted number.

"Really?" Alison kept saying after Casey filled her in.

"Of course, really," Casey told her. "It's funny, Alison, my parents and Mr. Robinson told me the same thing—to do positive things, not negative things, even though I thought I was doing something positive!"

"That's the real problem. You were thinking," Alison said.

Casey went on. "So now we're going to do something that is really positive, with no doubt about it."

There was a moment of silence. Then Alison replied warily, "Do what?"

"Something positive," Casey repeated. "Alison, is there anything in the whole world you'd rather do than help someone deserving?"

"Yes," Alison said. "To be perfectly honest, I'd rather meet Randolph Mantooth than do anything in the whole world."

"Be serious," Casey said.

"I am serious, both honest and serious."

"Listen!" Casey was so eager she bounced up and down, banging her elbow into the wall. "When I was thinking about doing positive things, I thought about Sylvia Schweppe."

"Who?"

"You know Sylvia—the one who works at the little Quick Shop. And I thought about what she said about not being able to afford to go back to school. Remember?"

There was another suspicious pause. "What about it?"

"Well, what if we raised some money to pay her tuition at the junior college and buy her books and anything else she'd need?"

"She said she didn't finish high school."

"That's all right. We can help her study for the GED test, so she can get the equivalent of a high school diploma. And after that she can go on to college and work to put herself through, and have a real career, with a job that she loves to go to every day."

"I don't know," Alison said. "I suppose we could ask her and see if she'd like that."

"Oh, no! We can't ask her," Casey said. "We want it to be a surprise!"

"How will we get the money?"

Casey thought a moment, and the idea hit her in a burst of inspiration. "We could have a garage sale!"

Alison sighed. "Okay. I'll go along with it, if you say so, Casey. But I've got this strange feeling that when you plan a surprise, it's going to turn out to be a surprise on us!"

4 | What Could Go Wrong?

Things weren't too bad at school during the next couple of days. Casey brought home an A on her history test. Mr. Robinson avoided her in the hallways. And the sixth-grade pest, Bucky Beaglemaster, stopped teasing her about being in trouble, when she informed him she was just a few dollars away from her first karate lesson, and would be looking for someone to practice on.

Casey and Alison began collecting things from their mothers for the garage sale, and storing them in the Cooper garage.

"This looks like a lot of junk," Alison said, holding up a slightly rusty corn-bread pan her mother had donated.

"But people buy these things," Casey said. She rubbed the back of her hand across her sweaty forehead, leaving a streak of dirt. "We haven't got enough stuff, you know. I'll phone Eugenia tonight when she gets home from work and see if she'll give us something. Can you think of anyone else?"

"Can we ask some of your neighbors?"

"I don't think they'll donate things and come to the sale both. I'd rather they came to the sale."

"Then how about my neighbors? A woman who lives down the street from us has a lot of interesting stuff in her house. She might donate something."

"Okay. Let's go," Casey said. She put down an old lampshade with yellow fringe around the bottom and wiped her hands on her jeans.

"I told you about her once," Alison said. "Her name is Rosalie Mertz. She used to be an airline stewardess a long, long time ago. And she's very tidy and has beautiful satin pillows on her chairs and a very, very clean house and . . ."

"Alison," Casey said, sighing dramatically, "if you want me to change my clothes and wash my face, just say so."

"So," Alison said.

"Be right back," Casey told her. In less than ten minutes she had pulled off her dirty clothes, left them in the middle of the bathroom floor, washed her face, and combed her hair. She put on a clean pair of jeans and a T-shirt that had printed on it The Only Way To Go Is d∩.

Alison was patiently waiting in the garage when Casey got back. As they walked to her house, Casey could smell the spicy fragrance of the Ligustrum blooms, which made her sneeze, but reminded her that summer vacation wasn't far off, and that was a great feeling!

"Stop jumping up and down like that," Alison said. "I'm trying to talk to you."

"I'm tired of talking about Randolph Mantooth," Casey said. "Why don't you fall in love with someone else?"

"Someday I probably will," Alison said logically. "Turn in here."

"What?" Casey stopped.

"In here. This is where Rosalie Mertz lives."

Casey looked at the white stucco house with the roof of curved red tiles. "I didn't know this was her house," she said. "I always liked this house."

"You'll like Mrs. Mertz, too," Alison said. "Come on."

She rang the bell, and in less than a minute a slender, gray-haired woman in an orange jogging suit threw the door open wide and smiled at them.

Alison introduced Casey and told Mrs. Mertz why they had come.

"Of course I can find something for you, but you

must call me Rosalie," the woman said. "Mrs. Mertz sounds too formal."

She waved them into her living room. Casey tripped on the fringe of a small throw rug and managed to land upright in a brocade chair.

"I'll get some soft drinks and something to munch on," Rosalie said. "Alison, tell Casey about the things in this room while I'm in the kitchen."

Casey stared as she looked around the room. She had never seen a room like this. There were framed photographs on the wall, and what looked like a large black shawl. Wood carvings and painted pottery figurines lined the mantel of the corner fireplace and filled every tabletop in the room.

"Souvenirs from her flights to Mexico," Alison said. "Remember? I told you Rosalie used to be a stewardess."

"She must have had a great time collecting all these," Casey said.

She picked up what looked like a small, one-sided clay Christmas tree, filled with brightly colored animals, people, flowers, and fruit.

Rosalie came through the doorway with some glasses on a tray and a plate of brownies. "I'm glad to have someone help me eat these," she said.

She put the tray on the floor and sat cross-legged beside it. "I really need another table in here," she added. "There isn't any room left on these."

"You must have traveled a lot in your lifetime," Casey said.

"Only when I was a stewardess," Rosalie told her. "After I got married and began raising a family, there never seemed to be enough money for long-distance travel." She handed Casey a glass. "Those days as a stewardess were something special. I worked for Atterbury Airlines in the thirties, in a twin-engine plane that held only ten people! Just ten people! Can you believe it?"

Casey smiled to see Rosalie's face shining with bright memories. "Did you do what stewardesses do now?" she asked.

"Not in quite the same way," Rosalie said. "We did try to make passengers happy, but we served them perfectly terrible meals of cold meat and potato salad, and lots of coffee. And the stewardesses had to be registered nurses."

"In case someone got sick?"

"We were supposed to be able to handle any emergency. Luckily nothing drastic happened on any of my flights." She sighed happily. "There was so much about the work that I loved."

"Why did you stop?" Casey asked.

Rosalie looked surprised. "Because I got married," she said. "Stewardesses had to be young and single and pretty."

"That's terrible!" Casey said indignantly. "It's il-legal!"

"And soon I had a family to raise." Rosalie sipped her drink and smiled at Alison, who reached for an-other brownie. "The airlines have changed the rule now. They have to keep a stewardess in her job after she gets married."

"And they don't call them 'stewardesses' anymore," Alison piped up. "They call them 'flight attendants.' At least they did on the flight we took to Iowa, to visit my grandmother last year."

"I wish I could do it all again," Rosalie said. "Being a stewardess—or flight attendant—is a terrific job."

Casey got excited. "Then why don't you apply for your job back?"

"At my age? They'd never hire me. Harvey Atter-bury still runs that airline, although he must be in his early seventies by this time. And I don't think he's changed a bit. He likes his stewardesses young and pretty."

"Oh!" Casey said indignantly. "He does, does he!"

Alison quickly stood up and pulled at Casey's arm. "Rosalie, it's been so nice visiting with you, but we must get back to work if we want to have our garage sale this weekend."

"Of course," Rosalie said. She stood up and jerked down the legs of her jogging suit. "I've got some things in the garage. If you girls come with me, we'll see what we can find."

Alison poked Casey as they followed, and whispered, "Don't get upset again. Keep your mind on the garage sale. We've got enough to do."

But Casey wasn't satisfied. "Rosalie," she said, "if you had a chance to go back to work as a flight attendant, would you take the job?"

"Would I?" Rosalie pushed open the back door with one hip. "You bet I would!"

"Let's get busy on the garage sale," Alison said quickly, as though she were trying to distract Casey.

Casey just smiled to herself. She had the beginning of an idea, but it could wait. Alison was right. This was the time to work on the garage sale and save the future for Sylvia Schweppe. Her idea about Rosalie Mertz's future would come later.

Rosalie had more to give them than either girl had imagined, so they struggled back and forth to Casey's garage three times, with as much in their arms as they could carry. "I think we've got enough for our sale, Casey," Alison said, her voice rising hopefully.

Casey rubbed her hands together and grinned. "We sure do! I'll make some signs, and we'll put them on the lawn and the corners, and you make some cards and put them in the nearest grocery stores. We'll have our sale this Saturday."

Alison laughed. "Sylvia is going to be so excited when we surprise her."

"Surprise who?"

Casey looked up to see Paul standing in the open garage doorway.

"Sylvia Schweppe," Casey said, and she told him the story.

"I ought to put you on a retainer, Casey," Paul said. "I just dropped by to tell you that my boss liked the interview I did with you and Mr. Robinson. And now it seems you may have another story for me."

"About the garage sale?"

"One step further. Suppose I go with you girls when you give Sylvia the money. I think it would be interesting to catch her reaction on film. Has she told you what she'd like to study?"

"All she told us," Alison said, "was that she hated her job and was there as a way to stay alive."

"Poor kid," Paul said.

"Well, she's not exactly a kid," Casey said. "But anyone can go back to school, Paul."

"You're right," he said. He handed Casey a business card. "Here are my phone numbers at the station and at home. Call me when you're ready for the big presentation."

"Thanks, Paul," Casey said. She turned to Alison after he had left. "This is going to be the biggest surprise Sylvia ever had in her whole life, I bet!"

"You know it," Alison said. "And it's not going to backfire, the way Mr. Robinson's surprise did." She paused. "Is it, Casey?"

The two girls looked at each other.

"Of course not," Casey said. "What could possibly go wrong?"

5 | One Surprise Too Many!

Saturday was a perfect day for a garage sale, with clear, almost smog-free skies; and the garage was filled with the fragrance of pans of Mrs. Cooper's gingerbread, still warm from the oven.

Casey put a high price on the gingerbread squares, and was doubly delighted to see that the gingerbread made people so thirsty, they bought cups of coffee from the big urn Eugenia had borrowed from a friend.

People from the neighborhood came, and shoppers arrived in cars. An old man in overalls was in the driveway when the sale began. He spent an hour examining every item, then finally bought one five-cent bent screwdriver and left with a big smile on his face.

A breathless woman, blond hair flying behind her,

dashed into the garage asking, "Any old books?" When the answer was "No," she dashed out just as quickly.

A fat woman, carrying a nasty-tempered Pekingese who barked at everyone, bought the lampshade with the yellowed fringe and a broken lawn mower.

"Why do people want this stuff?" Alison whispered to Casey.

But a woman interrupted by looking frantically around the garage and saying, "No orange-juice cans? No Popsicle sticks?"

"You want to buy used orange-juice cans and Popsicle sticks?" Casey asked in surprise. This was the strangest customer they'd had yet.

"Of course she does." Casey's mother had just come to the garage with a fresh pan of gingerbread, and she turned to the woman with a smile. "I've got a few orange-juice cans I've been saving to plant seedlings in, but I'll give them to you. Brownie leader?"

"Cub Scouts," the woman said. "You don't know how hard it is to collect the materials we need for the handicrafts part of the program."

"Oh, yes I do," Casey's mother said. "Bluebirds and Camp Fire Girls—three years."

The two women walked off toward the house, Mrs. Cooper explaining how to make wall plaques from old phonograph records.

Casey made change for a man who was buying a wig with long, flowing black hair. "It's not for me. It's for our little theater group," he said with a wink. "This is a real find. You don't have any clothes from the forties or fifties, do you?"

"We weren't born then," Alison said. "We don't know what they look like."

Casey got busy helping three little children with sticky gingerbread on their fingers peel off the pennies they had been clutching, so they could buy a comic book.

"Hi," a voice said close to her ear, and she looked up to see Gladys, the camera person.

"Paul sent me over to get some shots of the garage sale," she said. "Your gingerbread is too expensive."

"Law of supply and demand," Casey said. "You want a piece?"

Gladys sniffed. "It's for a good cause," she said, and she pulled some change from her pocket.

Casey put the largest piece of gingerbread on a napkin, while Gladys took some moving shots of the garage and the people in it.

Some of them stared at Gladys, while others ignored her. A man in his old gardening clothes looked around the garage carefully. "What's this all about?" he asked. "Are we in a movie or something?"

"Watch your Channel 12 newscasts," Gladys said,

swinging her camera down and biting into the gingerbread in one smooth motion.

Gladys waved good-bye, and after a few hours the crowd thinned to a trickle of customers.

"We're going to get stuck with some of this stuff," Casey said to Alison. "I hate to sit here all day trying to get rid of a photograph of an erupting volcano in a frame made of seashells and a plaster elephant holding an ashtray in his trunk. How much money have we got?"

Alison opened the cigar box and counted it. "Eighty-five dollars," she said.

"We've got plenty," Casey said. "There's enough there for Sylvia's student-body fees and all the textbooks she'll have to buy for a couple of semesters."

"And when we sell the rest of this . . ." Alison began, but Casey shook her head.

"We're through," she said.

"Your mother and father won't like it if we leave these things in the garage," Alison said.

Casey watched a young man climb out of his beat-up car and slouch up the sidewalk. "Here comes a customer," she said. "We'll see how much we can get rid of."

"Hey," the man mumbled as he came into the garage, blinking in the dimmer light. He began to look at the items on the nearest table, but he stopped, raised his head, and sniffed. "What smells so good?" he asked.

"Gingerbread that used to be here," Casey said. "It's all gone."

"My bad luck," the man said.

"No, it isn't!" Casey said. "This is your good-luck day! Have an absolutely free cup of coffee." She hurried around the table to the coffee urn, and managed to get from the dregs over half a paper cup of coffee before the spigot stopped dripping.

"Thanks," the man said. He took a sip and made a face. "Your coffee is terrible."

"That's why it's free," Alison said.

Casey spoke up quickly. "It's not the only thing that's free," she said.

"Yeah? What else is free?"

"What are you looking for?" Casey asked.

"Some dishes for the place I live in," he said. "You got anything to eat on? They don't have to match."

"As a matter of fact, we do," Alison said. "A couple of plates are a little bit chipped, though. Does that matter?"

"Well . . ." he began.

"The chipped ones are free," Casey said.

"Okay by me," he told them.

"And with the dishes, as a bonus gift, you get this beautiful plaster elephant holding an ashtray."

42

He made a strangling noise as he stared at the elephant Casey thrust into his hands. "It's the worst-looking art I ever saw," he said. "I love it."

"You love it?"

"Yeah. It's awful. I really love it. You got any more junk like this?"

"I've been saving the best news for last," Casey said. "With your purchase of the dishes, you get everything left in the garage sale—including the elephant you love. Come on. We'll help you load it in your car."

"Wait a minute," he said. "What will I do with it?"

"No problem," Casey said. "You can take your time sorting through it, maybe finding some presents for people you like—or don't like. And when you get through the sorting, you can have a garage sale yourself, and make lots of money."

"I didn't exactly figure on this," the man said. But Casey had already begun handing him things. She slipped an old fishing hat on his head and picked up the photograph of the volcano framed in seashells.

He smiled at her over the top of his armload of things. "Hey! That's a really awful picture frame. I love it!"

"See," Casey said. "You'll find all sorts of good stuff in here when you get home."

"Well, okay," the man said. "I really do love that picture frame. It's bad! Fantastic!"

"What are you going to do with this awful stuff you love?" Alison asked as she struggled down the driveway with the last armload of garage-sale leftovers.

"Decorate my place," the man said. "It's going to look really weird. I'm going to love it."

They watched him drive away, and Casey grinned at Alison. "Here. You carry the money box, and I'll call Paul. We're ready to give Sylvia her big surprise."

"*You* carry the money box and call Paul," Alison said, pushing the box back to her. "I'm going home to take a bath and change if we're going to be on television."

"Oh, Alison, why do you have to get all dressed up just because we'll be on the news program?" Casey asked. "That will take too long."

"No, it won't," Alison said. "I'll hurry. I promise. I couldn't think of looking like this if Randolph Mantooth saw me."

"What's Randolph Mantooth got to do with all this?" Casey asked.

"He must watch the news on television," Alison said. "He might watch this station. And he might see me. So don't argue with me, Casey. I'll meet you in front of the grocery store, and I bet I get there before you and Paul do."

Casey went inside the house and counted the money again, just to make sure it was all there. She had forgotten to charge the last customer for the dishes, but she shrugged. It was worth it to get rid of all the junk her parents would have wanted out of their garage sooner or later—and probably sooner. Now she was free to carry out the rest of the plan.

Casey could hear her mother and father in the den, talking about new drapes, so Casey didn't bother them. She called Paul, found him in, and arranged to meet him in half an hour in front of the grocery store.

Casey took time to eat an apple and a stack of graham crackers, washing everything down with a glass of milk. She looked at the kitchen clock, jumped up from the table, and jogged to the grocery store.

"Darn!" she mumbled. Alison was already standing off to one side, where Sylvia couldn't see her from the plate glass window, and she was wearing her new blouse and favorite skirt. "She did beat us here!"

Casey joined Alison, who couldn't help looking smug, and in a couple of minutes Paul and Gladys arrived.

"I take it the garage sale was a success?" Paul asked.

"The gingerbread was overpriced," Gladys said. "But good," she added.

"I thought your sale would take a couple of days," Paul said.

"Everything moved fast," Casey told him.

"Especially with the last customer," Alison said.

"Are you girls ready for the surprise?" Paul asked.

"Ready," Casey said. She began to get so excited she bounced up and down on her toes. "What shall we do?"

"Let's get inside the store," Paul said. "Gladys can begin shooting then."

"It's an awfully small store," Alison said.

"We'll have enough room," Paul told her.

They entered the store—Casey and Alison first, Paul and Gladys following. Sylvia looked up, startled.

"What's going on?" she gasped. She stood up and clutched the edge of the checkout counter, staring at Gladys' camera. "Hey, wait!" she yelled, shielding her face with one arm.

"You're on television!" Alison shouted.

"No!" Sylvia screamed. "Turn it off! Take those lights away!"

Paul tried to be helpful. He stepped around the counter, stood close to her and put a hand on her shoulder. He held the microphone up and said, "Sylvia Schweppe, these young ladies, Casey Cooper and Alison Engleman, discovered you and what you are doing, and they've taken steps to change your whole life!"

Sylvia threw both hands up in the air and began to sob. "I don't know how you did it! How did you find out? I thought my disguise was good enough to fool anyone!"

"Sylvia," Casey yelled, tugging at Sylvia's upraised arm. "Calm down! We're here to talk about some money!"

"I don't know where the money is!" Sylvia cried. "I only drove the car! Mac's got the money stashed somewhere near San Diego!"

6 | Not Another Good Idea!

Paul didn't lose his command of the situation for a moment. He seemed to make his voice a little deeper, a little firmer, and he said, "Sylvia, you might begin by telling us your real name."

"Audrey Flummer," she hiccupped.

"And Audrey, you drove the car during the holdup of . . ."

"The San Diego International Savings and Loan Company." Sylvia sniffled and wiped her eyes on her sleeve. "That stupid Mac said I wouldn't get caught! I was just supposed to bleach my hair and lie low in this stupid job and wait while Mac works on another caper. Then when it's safe, we were supposed to get together and split the money! Stupid!"

Paul put a knowledgeable look on his face and spoke earnestly into the camera. "Today Casey Cooper and Alison Engleman planned a surprise for their friend, Sylvia Schweppe, who was unhappy in her job in this small grocery store. They held a garage sale to raise money to send Sylvia back to school, but now to their surprise, they've found that Sylvia is really Audrey Flummer in disguise, hiding out for her part in a bank robbery."

"Huh?" Audrey said, her red-rimmed eyes flicking from Paul to the girls and back to Paul.

"In a few moments Audrey Flummer will meet with the district attorney . . ."

"Hey! Wait a minute!" she interrupted.

". . . where she'll find that everything will go easier for her because of her cooperation in locating the other members of the gang."

"You mean you *didn't* find out who I was?" Sylvia groaned.

"This is Paul Baker, Channel 12 News, Los Angeles."

Sylvia slumped onto the stool. "That stupid Mac!" she mumbled.

"Okay, Gladys," Paul said. "That's enough film. I'll get in touch with the police, and you rush that film in. We can probably use it in a special newsbreak."

Gladys shifted her camera and turned to Casey. "Seeing how everything worked out, can I have back the money I gave you for that overpriced ginger-bread?"

"Move, Gladys!" Paul said.

"The whole world is crazy," Gladys muttered as she pushed through the doorway.

Paul dialed the phone on the wall. Sylvia leaned on the counter near him with her head in her hands.

"Don't be upset," Casey said. "Look, Sylvia . . . Audrey." She held out the box. "We've already raised some money for your defense fund."

Audrey took the box and peered inside. It seemed to make her feel worse, because she started to cry all over again.

"If Mac's as stupid as you said and made up the plan, and you followed it, then you could always plead insanity," Casey added helpfully.

"He'll have to see this news special," Alison whispered to Casey.

"Mac?"

"No, Randolph Mantooth. I feel sorry for Audrey. I really do. Well, I guess I feel as sorry as anyone would feel for a bank robber, which isn't terribly sorry. But on the other hand, I'm glad I changed clothes, because I'm sure now that Randolph Mantooth is going to see me."

"Can't you think about anything else?" Casey asked.

"Yes," Alison said, "but not right now."

It didn't take long for the police to arrive. Soon afterward, the owner of the Quick Shop showed up. He was so upset he kept biting his fingernails. And as suddenly as they had arrived, everyone left. The little store was padlocked, and Paul was telling Casey and Alison they were terrific.

"I'll drop by your house in time to watch the newscast tonight, if you think Eugenia might be there," he added.

"She probably will be if I call her office and tell her what happened," Casey said. "Except I don't feel like telling anyone. One more good idea down the drain."

"Then I'll phone her," Paul said. At the moment, Casey didn't care a bit. She said good-bye to Alison and walked home alone, one slow step at a time.

When she entered her house her mother greeted her happily. "Was Sylvia Schweppe surprised?" she asked.

"She sure was," Casey said.

"Did she say what she was interested in studying?"

"Crime," Casey said glumly.

Her mother looked at her carefully. "I think there's something you need to tell me."

"Could it wait until the newscast?" Casey asked. "You'll see it all then."

"If that's what you want," she began. Then her eyes widened. "Casey! You weren't photographed for television like that, were you? Oh, no! Not in old jeans and a T-shirt that says Be Nice to Me. I'm One of a Kind!"

"Mother, it doesn't matter," Casey said.

"But everyone in the whole city will be watching that newscast!"

"Even Randolph Mantooth?"

"Who?"

"Never mind, Mom. I was just thinking about Alison. If it's all right with you, I think I'll take a bath and change clothes."

"All right with me? *Now* you want to take a bath? Casey!"

Casey left her mother talking to herself, and tried to get things into perspective as she soaked in a hot tub. She had attempted to do something positive, and everyone had told her it was negative. Then she had tried to do something else that was positive, and it had gone wrong. She was determined to prove she could actually do something right.

Casey's mood didn't improve that evening. The newscast only made it worse. Her mother took one look at Casey on camera in her dirty T-shirt and jeans and burst into tears. Her father had discovered that his fishing hat had been sold in the garage sale and scowled at everyone. And Eugenia kept saying, "Casey, if you had to uncover a gang of bank robbers, why did you have to pick on the *woman* in the gang?"

Paul was the only one who was happy. He watched

Marsha, the anchor person, lead into his film, and grinned at himself on TV.

Somehow he talked Eugenia into going to a movie with him, and some neighbors invited Casey's parents to come over and play cards.

"What about you, Casey?" her mother asked. "Are you going to be alone here tonight? Couldn't you have a friend over?"

"I'd rather be alone," Casey said.

Her mother wrapped her arms around her. "Dear heart," she said. "Don't be so unhappy. We're very proud of you for catching the getaway driver of that robbery. Just think, you solved the case!"

"If you're so proud of me, why did you cry?" Casey asked.

"She cried because she gets sentimental over old T-shirts, and because her conscience has bothered her ever since she threw out my favorite fishing hat!" her father answered.

Mrs. Cooper gave a long sigh. "Are you sure you don't mind being alone?"

"I'll call Alison," Casey said.

"That takes care of your evening," her father said. "We'll be home before you hang up."

She watched them leave, then she phoned Alison.

Alison answered in such a musical, unusual voice that Casey said, "Hey, is that you?"

"Oh," Alison said. "I hoped . . ."

"Randolph Mantooth is not going to call you," Casey said. She felt so mean she quickly added, "Even if you did look great on television."

"Really Casey? You think I looked great?"

"Yes," Casey said. "You looked better than anybody else in the whole news program."

She heard Alison's little giggle of contentment, and she sighed. "Can you come over?"

"No," Alison said. "I'm baby-sitting my little brother. My parents told me to get to bed early because we're going to visit my grandparents tomorrow. I'll see you Monday."

Casey felt a lot better talking to her best friend. "Okay," she said. "Is it all right if I come over to your house after school Monday? We may want to visit Rosalie."

There was a pause. "I guess so, Casey, if we just eat something and talk about interesting things. But that's all."

"What's the matter, Alison? Don't you trust me?"

"I know you well enough to figure out that you're thinking up an idea, Casey. The answer is no."

"You haven't even heard it yet," Casey said. "See you Monday." As she put down the phone she smiled. The answer might be no right now, but just wait until Alison heard the idea! This one was bound to work!

7 | Casey's Challenge

On Monday afternoon Casey changed into her jeans and a T-shirt on which was printed People Like Me Are Hard To Replace, and went with Alison to Rosalie's house. She was careful not to trip over Rosalie's rug, and she sat in one of the brocade chairs as gracefully as she could.

"Iced tea?" Rosalie said, and she hurried to the kitchen without waiting for an answer.

Casey closed her eyes for a moment and thought about the fragrance of the room. People's houses smelled differently. This room was a little spicy. Her own living room smelled of pine oil, and Eugenia's apartment had a slightly woodsy fragrance of potted plants and damp soil.

"You're not going to sleep, are you?" Alison whispered.

Casey's eyelids flipped open. "I'm thinking," she said.

"I hate it when you think," Alison said. "I mean . . . I know you think, but . . ." She put her hands to her face, giggling.

Casey laughed too, and Rosalie beamed at them as she entered the room, putting the familiar tray of glasses in the same place on the floor.

"I should have come to your garage sale and bought a table," Rosalie said.

"We didn't have any tables," Casey said. "We had a lot of weird things, like an elephant holding an ashtray."

"I know about the elephant," Rosalie said. "I gave it to you."

"Oh-oh," Casey said. "I'm sorry." She tried not to notice Alison glaring at her.

"That was an ugly elephant," Rosalie said, handing the girls their glasses of iced tea. "One of my regular passengers gave that elephant to me, and it went right into the garage. I couldn't stand looking at it." She smiled and stared off at something the girls couldn't see. "Those days were great fun," she added. "I especially enjoyed the flights from Los Angeles to Mexico and back."

"Would you like to do it again?" Casey asked. She hurried to add, before Alison could open her mouth, "Because if you do, we could try to get you hired again."

"I don't think you'd succeed," Rosalie said. "I'm too old to be a flight attendant—in management's opinion."

"How about your opinion?"

"I'd love it. I'm in great health, my two sons are both grown and living with their families in other cities, so I have no responsibilities. And I'm getting awfully tired of just living on my late husband's pension and doing volunteer work."

Casey jumped up from the chair. "Then we'll do it!"

"You keep saying, 'we,'" Alison said. "Are you thinking of making me a part of that 'we,' Casey Cooper?"

"We need you, Alison," Casey said. "Don't you see what a wonderful thing this will be for Rosalie, to get her old job back? You wouldn't desert me, would you?"

Alison groaned. "I suppose not."

Casey patted Alison's shoulder. "I knew I could count on you." She turned to Rosalie. "If it's all right with you, Rosalie, I'll phone the president of Atterbury Airlines, and tell him you'll be in to see him."

Rosalie hopped up from her cross-legged position on

the floor. "It's probably impossible, but I can't wait to hear what Harvey Atterbury is going to say! We used to be such good friends! Oh, Casey! Alison! This is going to be such fun!"

It didn't take Casey long to find the phone number for Atterbury Airlines in the Yellow Pages. She dialed the number, then realized that she hadn't thought of what to say. She took a deep breath. Well, she was supposed to think positive thoughts, so she'd keep the conversation on a positive level.

As soon as the woman on the switchboard answered, Casey said, "May I please speak to the president of Atterbury Airlines?"

There was a pause. "One moment, and I'll connect you with his secretary."

Casey put her hand over the mouthpiece of the phone. "I have to get through the secretary first."

"Tell her you're calling for Rosalie Mertz," Rosalie whispered. Her nose was pink with excitement. "That ought to get old Harvey!"

A formal voice suddenly said, "May I help you?"

"I'm calling for one of your former flight attendants," Casey said. "Rosalie Mertz. Could we talk to the president of Atterbury Airlines, please?"

"Is this a business call?"

"Business and pleasure," Casey said. "Rosalie is one of his old friends."

There was a moment of indecision; then the woman

said, "He's just coming out of his office. One moment, please, while I ask him if he'll take the call."

Casey held her breath until finally a voice boomed into the telephone, "I don't know any Rosalie Mertz!"

"Is this the president of Atterbury Airlines?" Casey gasped.

"Of course it is."

"Well, Rosalie Mertz used to be one of your flight attendants, and she wants to talk to you about getting her job back." Casey's voice lost a great deal of its confidence.

"If she meets the age, height and weight qualifications, she can apply through channels," he growled. "Just don't bother me."

"You don't have an age limit, do you?" Casey asked, a little more bravely. "I mean, you can't discriminate and . . ."

He interrupted. "How old is this Rosalie . . . whatever her name is?"

"Rosalie Mertz, and she's, well . . . sort of over sixty. . . ."

"Sixty-five," Rosalie prompted.

But the voice simply said, "You're crazy! Tell her she's crazy too!" And there was the thump of a receiver being slammed into its cradle.

Casey put down the telephone and repeated the conversation to the others.

"What a rude man!" Alison was indignant.

"That doesn't sound like Harvey Atterbury," Rosalie said. "He was always a very friendly person. Maybe he's gotten to be crabby in his old age."

"Well, he certainly has no right to be so rude," Alison said.

"He has no right to discriminate either," Casey said. "Just because Rosalie isn't a sex object."

"I think we should simply forget about it," Rosalie said.

"I don't," Casey said. "There's more than one way of getting things done."

"Now, Casey," Alison began.

But Casey added, "I'm going to talk to Paul!"

8 | A Warning!

When Casey arrived home, Alison with her, the house was filled with the deep, rich aroma of pot roast.

"Mom," Casey said, finding her mother peeling potatoes in the kitchen, "why aren't you practicing your typing?"

"Because I'm making dinner," she answered.

"Daddy should be making dinner," she said.

Her father came into the room behind her. "Why should I have to make dinner? I work in an office. Your mother works in the home. We divide chores that way."

"But, Dad," Casey said, trying to be patient. "Mom is learning typing so she can expand her horizons.

Then she'll have an office job, too, and you'll have to learn to cook so you can take turns."

"I have an even better idea," Mr. Cooper said. He took his wife's hand and pulled her away from the sink. He put the paring knife in Casey's right hand. "Since there are three of us, it would be even more fair to divide the cooking job three ways. It might be good for you to begin learning right now."

"I know how to peel potatoes," Casey said.

"Then you'll agree it's a good job distribution?"

"I guess so." Casey gave a sigh and turned to the sink.

"I think you lost that one," Alison said, as Casey's parents left the kitchen.

"Basically, my father is right," Casey said, working hard to keep too much potato from staying with the peeling.

"I'm going to learn to cook," Alison said, leaning on the kitchen counter, resting her chin in her hands. "I'm going to be a great cook, and I can make all sorts of good things to eat for Randolph." She sighed. "Do you think I'll ever meet him, Casey?"

Casey let what was left of the potato plop into the pan of water. "It's not too likely," she said.

"But if I do meet him, will he notice me? As my very best friend, tell me the truth."

Casey turned and smiled at Alison. "As your very

best friend, I can tell you that he's bound to notice you, especially if you're introduced to him. He might think he's a little too old for you, but . . ." She hurried to add, as she saw the pucker in Alison's forehead, "But you can talk him out of that idea, right?"

"Right," Alison said.

"So now that's settled, and we can talk about calling Paul."

"Do we have to?"

"Yes. Unless you think we should talk to Eugenia first."

Mrs. Cooper popped back into the kitchen and in a low voice said, "I just wanted to make sure you knew what you were doing, and that you put salt in the water. You have to put a half-teaspoon of salt in the water or the potatoes taste flat, and Eugenia and Paul happen to be coming to dinner."

"Great!" Casey said.

"I think so," her mother said. "They really make a very nice couple."

"Mom!" Casey said. "Eugenia isn't going to marry Paul!"

"What's wrong with Eugenia marrying Paul?" her mother said.

"Eugenia is a career woman. She doesn't want to get married for years. She told me so."

"Most of us don't exactly plan when we're going to fall in love."

Alison smiled. "That's nice. Eugenia and Paul."

"Yeech!" Casey sputtered.

"There they are now," her mother said, listening to the voices in the living room. She took the knife from Casey's hand. "I'll finish these in a minute. You go in and say hello." She threw a warning glance at Casey. "And don't mention what we were talking about."

Casey scuffed her way into the living room. She nodded at Paul, prepared to begin disliking him for trying to rearrange her aunt's plans, but Paul held out two boxes of saltwater taffy.

"It's a present for you girls," he said. "I got a raise, thanks to that film story about Sylvia."

Casey thanked him and stuffed a taffy into her mouth, chewing carefully so she wouldn't pull out her fillings. "Paul, I'm glad you're here," she said, completely forgetting about whatever feelings Paul had for Eugenia. And she told him about Rosalie and the disappointing telephone conversation with the president of Atterbury Airlines.

"Hmmm," Paul said. "I like the idea. An interview with Rosalie might make a very good story."

"It's not just the story, Paul," Eugenia broke in. "It's the basic concept of a woman's right to be useful in her profession, regardless of her age, as long as she's able to do her job well."

Casey clapped her hands. "That was great!" she said to Eugenia.

68

Eugenia smiled. "Equal job opportunity for women is what I'm working so hard for, Casey."

"Is something like that hereditary?" Alison asked, nibbling on her taffy.

"Can we go to see Rosalie, Paul?" Casey tugged at his arm.

"Wait until after dinner." Her father came into the room. "Doris will have it ready in just a few minutes."

Eugenia shook her head. "When are you going to release Doris from the kitchen, John?"

"After she's washed the dishes," he said.

Eugenia had her mouth open to answer, but he quickly added, "This dinner was a cooperative venture, Eugenia. We all helped."

"Really?" She looked pleased.

"Yes. Doris did a couple of little things that had to be done. I came in and tasted the gravy, and Casey peeled the potato."

"Potatoes." Eugenia corrected him with a sigh.

"Just one potato," Casey mumbled. "It takes longer to peel a potato than I thought."

Mrs. Cooper called everyone to the table, and Casey's interest zeroed in on the pot roast.

After dinner, Paul, Casey and Alison phoned Rosalie, and she was excited about the prospect of being interviewed on TV. "How about after the girls get home from school tomorrow?" she asked Paul. "They ought to be on hand too."

"Fine," Paul said. "I'll be there with the photographer."

At school the next morning, Alison smoothed down the skirt of her dress, her cheeks rosy with excitement, and gave an oral report on What It's Like Seeing Yourself on the Television News.

When it was Casey's turn to stand before the class, she gave everyone time to read her T-shirt, which said The Princess Who Kissed A Frog Got Nothing But Warts, and spoke for five minutes about Job Inequalities for Women in Auto Repair Shops.

Both girls were out on the sidewalk in front of the school almost before the dismissal bell finished ringing. They raced each other to Rosalie's home. The Channel 12 car was parked in front of the house, and they hurried to ring the doorbell.

Rosalie ushered them inside the living room. "I wouldn't let them start until you got here," she said.

Casey waved at Gladys, who nodded, smiled, and adjusted her lights and camera.

"I tried to get the Atterbury Airlines president to give me a statement," Paul said, "but his secretary said he had no comment." He moved Rosalie and the girls to a spot in front of the fireplace, where some of Rosalie's souvenirs served as a background. In his resonant television voice he gave a little of the story. Then he smiled at Rosalie. Gladys was busy filming.

70

"So you think you'd like to fly again in your old job as stewardess?" he asked her.

Her eyes sparkled. "They are called flight attendants now," she said. "And you bet I'd like to be a flight attendant again. I was a very good one."

"I understand that you're thinking of applying again to Atterbury Airlines?"

Rosalie shrugged. "Casey phoned the president of Atterbury Airlines. He said he didn't remember me, which is a surprise, because we used to be friends and sent each other Christmas cards for years and years."

Casey found herself telling Paul and the microphone about her conversation with the president of the airline. Then Alison, in a breathy voice, added a statement of support for what Rosalie wanted to do, and the conversation was over.

"That's it," Paul said. "Thank you, ladies."

Casey blinked, adjusting to the normal lighting in the room. "Will that be on tonight, Paul?"

"That's right," he said. "Unless it gets bumped for some world-shaking news event. Tune in at ten and watch yourselves on television. This is going to be a good story and will probably draw letters and phone calls from our viewers."

"Terrific!" Casey said. "You think lots of people will support Rosalie?"

"I didn't say that," Paul said. "There will be some

for her, and some against her, and even a crank call or two. We always get a few crank calls."

"If there's a crank call, it will probably be from the president of Atterbury Airlines." Alison giggled.

Rosalie clasped her hands. "This is fun!" she said. "I can't wait to see us all on television!"

That night Casey sat on the floor in front of the set, hugging her knees. She felt great. The interview with Rosalie went well, and the whole family was attentive except her mother, who gave a little moan and mumbled something about that awful T-shirt and Alison's nice dress, until Eugenia put her hand over her sister's mouth.

As the interview ended and the commercial began, Eugenia said, "That was fantastic, Casey! I think something good is going to come out of this."

"I doubt it," Mr. Cooper said. "When I fly, I don't think of a grandmother-type taking care of me."

"Why not?" Casey asked. "Most people have nice thoughts about their grandmothers. Every time I see my grandmothers, they make me feel a little pampered and special."

"Say!" Eugenia said. "I think you've got the makings of a marvelous idea, Casey. Pampered and Special—Our Grandmother Service. How does that sound to you?"

The phone rang. Casey jumped up and raced to answer it. It was probably Alison.

But the voice was deep. And it was a disguised voice. Casey could tell that someone was trying to change the way he sounded. She frowned as she tried to place the voice, but she couldn't.

"Keep you nose out of other people's business, little girl," it said.

"But . . ." Casey began, ready to argue.

"You can take this as a warning," the man interrupted. He hung up with a bang.

Casey slowly placed the receiver on the cradle and went back to join the others.

"What's the matter?" her mother asked quickly. "There's something wrong, isn't there, Casey?"

Casey took a deep breath. Her mother always seemed to know almost what she was thinking. Well, she couldn't tell them about the threat, or they'd insist that she stop the plan to help Rosalie get her job back. And for all she knew, it was one of the bank robbers, still angry about what had happened with Sylvia.

"What's wrong, Casey?" her mother repeated.

"Oh, nothing," Casey said, flopping on the floor and managing a little laugh. "Would you believe that someone didn't like my T-shirt?"

She thought they'd recognize the joke and laugh, but her mother took the remark seriously and said, "I knew people would start to talk about those awful T-shirts!"

74

Eugenia jumped into the conversation, both of them distracted for the moment. Casey stared at her feet and thought again about the phone call. Someone was giving her a warning. Why? What would happen if she didn't take it?

9 | Casey Won't Give Up

At school the next day Mr. Robinson growled at Casey, as she passed him in the hallway, "I see you're trying to make trouble for someone else."

Casey stopped and shifted her books to the other arm. "Mr. Robinson, you yourself told me to do something positive. I'm just trying to help Rosalie Mertz get her job back."

"But stewardesses are supposed to be young and pretty! What you're doing is against all the rules!"

"What rules?"

The voice was sharp. Casey turned to see the music teacher, tall, stately Miss Dionetti, standing behind her. She was staring at Mr. Robinson as though he had hit a flat note at the choral program.

"Maybe you haven't flown lately, Mr. Robinson," Miss Dionetti said in her low, musical voice that carried the length of the hallway. "If you had, you'd have found that many of the flight attendants are male."

Mr. Robinson sputtered and took a step backward. "Now, Miss Dionetti, there is no reason to make an issue of this. I was just having a friendly conversation with Casey about . . ."

"I saw the television news last night too," Miss Dionetti said. "And I'm very proud of Casey. But back to the matter of 'pretty' flight attendants . . ."

Casey eased away and hurried down the hallway as fast as she could walk, trying not to trip over her own feet. She was glad that people had watched the television news, and she hoped that some of them would be on her side, as Miss Dionetti was. It would be terrific if Rosalie could get her job back.

Alison enjoyed being a minor celebrity, and spent hours telling everyone who asked, and a few who didn't, what it was like being interviewed for a news program. Casey, on the other hand, thought about Eugenia's slogan for grandmother service on Atterbury Airlines, and tried to think of ways she could use this idea to help Rosalie get her job back. She wasn't paying attention when she was called on in history, and she zonked out of math altogether. When Bucky Beaglemaster punched her arm, she stomped on his foot in a very halfhearted way. No one in the school was happier than Casey when the dismissal bell rang.

"Let's go to Rosalie's," she said to Alison, grabbing her arm and pulling her along the hallway. "We've got to find out if she heard anything from anyone at Atterbury Airlines!"

They arrived at Rosalie's house out of breath. Alison had no sooner pressed the doorbell, when Rosalie, dressed in a frilly blouse and flowered skirt, opened the door. There was something different about her, Casey thought.

"Come in!" she cried, her smile bright enough to make violets bloom. "An old friend is here. I want you girls to meet him!"

She led them into the living room and turned that smile on the small thin man who sat on the sofa, looking like a wire coil that was set to snap up without a moment's notice.

"Harvey Atterbury, of Atterbury Airlines," she said. "And these young ladies are Casey Cooper and Alison Engleman."

"You're the president of Atterbury Airlines?" Casey gasped.

The voice she heard was not the one that had barked at her that she was crazy. "No, I'm not, and you should get your facts straight before accusing someone!" He tried to look cross, but a smile got in the way. "You were talking to my son-in-law, Rodney Ditt-

man. He's the president of the airline. I'm the chairman of the board."

"Oh!" Casey said. "I'm sorry. I thought . . ."

"No harm done," he answered. "It was a lot of fun to see Lydia—that's my daughter—give Rodney a bad time." He chuckled. "And it gave me a good excuse to look up Rosalie again."

Rosalie sat beside him on the sofa and motioned the girls into chairs. "We've been having a lovely talk about the days when we flew down to Mexico and back."

Casey perched on the edge of her chair, leaning eagerly toward Mr. Atterbury. "Are you going to give Rosalie her job back?" she asked.

"Of course not," he said. "Rosalie's too old for that kind of work." He winked at her. "You should have seen her when she was younger. I always thought she had great legs."

Casey held her breath, waiting to see what would happen next, but Rosalie simply stretched out her legs and said, "Thank you, Harvey. They're still good-looking legs."

"Huh?" Casey gasped.

But Alison said, "This is so romantic and exciting! Tell us about your flights into Mexico."

"No!" Casey said, surprising herself by the urgency in her voice. "We need to talk about Rosalie's job."

"But we can't give her a job," Harvey said.

Casey looked at him carefully. "I hope you'll think about it."

"I don't want to think about it!" he shouted.

Rosalie put a hand on his arm. "Let's forget about it for now," she said.

"That's a good idea. Forget about it," Harvey said. "I don't know what's wrong with women today. They all think they have to be doing something they shouldn't . . . like Lydia. She's always butting into the business end of Atterbury Airlines. Thinks she has better management ideas than Rodney has."

"Maybe she's right," Casey said. "Atterbury Airlines isn't a very big airline. Maybe Lydia has ideas to make it grow."

"Why should it grow?" Harvey seemed to jump up and down inside himself, and Casey was afraid he would suddenly spring into the air. "We get enough business to keep it going."

"But if Lydia had better ideas?"

Harvey laughed. "What would a woman know about running an airline?"

Casey had her mouth open to answer, but she felt Alison tugging at her, and she saw Rosalie leaning toward her with a very pointed look, so she closed it.

"We have to go now," Alison said, pulling Casey to her feet.

"How nice," Rosalie said. "I mean, how nice you could come. Do come back for cookies someday."

81

There was a flurry of good-byes, and Casey found herself on the sidewalk, in front of Rosalie's house, facing Alison.

"We should have tried to convince him," Casey said.

"There are other ways of convincing people without hitting them on the head," Alison said.

"Hmmm," Casey said. "That reminds me. Speaking of hitting people on the head, I don't understand why Rosalie didn't get mad at Mr. Atterbury when he said she had good legs."

"Mr. Atterbury is Rosalie's friend, Casey. She likes him," Alison said. She began to walk toward her house.

"We'll just have to think of another way to get things done," Casey said, catching up to her friend. "I don't want to give up."

"Somebody might make you give up," Alison said.

"Who?" Casey's voice was barely a whisper. Had Alison got a warning phone call too?

But Alison had stopped and was laughing. "Why, Mr. Atterbury, Casey. That's who."

No, Alison wouldn't get a phone call like that. Her family had an unlisted phone number. And Casey certainly didn't want Alison to know about that warning. That might put an end to all her plans. She shivered.

"Why are you looking like that?" Alison asked her. "What are you thinking about?"

"Nothing," Casey answered. "Let's see what your mother has for us to eat." She didn't even want to admit to herself that she was more than a little bit scared.

10 | Casey Finds an Ally

Casey could hear the slow, uneven *click-tap* of the typewriter keys as she entered her house late that afternoon. She went back to the den to talk to her mother.

"It's discouraging," she sighed, dropping into the nearest chair.

"It certainly is," Mrs. Cooper said, staring at the keyboard.

"I mean, trying to get Atterbury Airlines to hire Rosalie. Mr. Atterbury was at her house this afternoon, and all they wanted to talk about was their old trips to Mexico."

Her mother shook her head. "Maybe you should forget your idea."

Casey sat up straight. "Don't even think that, Mom! I

wouldn't give up trying to get Rosalie her job back any more than you would give up your new career!"

"Career?" her mother said in a strangled voice, but Casey continued.

"In fact, Mom, I'll make dinner tonight, and that will give you more time to practice your typing. What are we having?"

"I planned to make beef stroganoff. I've got some sirloin and some fresh mushrooms and . . ."

"Would it be all right with you if we had hot dogs?" Casey asked. "I know how to make hot dogs."

The doorbell rang, and Casey jumped up. "Keep typing, Mom! I'll get it."

She hurried down the hall and opened the front door. Paul stood there.

"Hi," he said. "May I come in? I've got some good news for you."

"Sure," Casey said. She led him to a chair in the living room.

Paul looked around the room. "Eugenia doesn't happen to be here, does she?"

Casey shook her head. "She's at her office right now. I don't think she's coming over tonight. What's the good news you wanted to tell me?"

"It's about that spot on television about Rosalie," Paul said. "We've had a better phone response to that story than to anything we've ever done."

Casey immediately felt better. She perked up in her

chair and said, "Tell me about it! Were people for or against Rosalie? What did they say?"

"Mostly they were for her," Paul said. "Oh, there were a few people who got angry about the whole thing. A few wouldn't leave their names—we call those crank calls—and one caller sputtered so much we couldn't tell what he was saying. But there were so many calls in support of Rosalie Mertz getting her old job back that we think it deserves a follow-up story."

"Really?" Casey bounced up and down on the edge of her chair. "What kind of a follow-up?"

"I'm here to talk over some ideas with you," Paul said. "What do you think of interviewing the president of Atterbury Airlines? I could make another try at it."

Casey thought a moment. "How about interviewing his wife?"

She told Paul about Harvey Atterbury's visit to Rosalie that afternoon, and what he had said. "Maybe Lydia Dittman will help us."

"Not a bad idea," Paul said. He made some notes on a pad he pulled from his pocket. "Anything else you might have in mind?"

"Eugenia had a good idea," she said. "She thought of a slogan: Pampered and Special—Our Grandmother Service. What do you think about that?"

"I think Eugenia is terrific," Paul said. He made another note on his pad. "I'll stop by her apartment this evening and talk about the slogan with her. There's no telling how we could use something like that."

"Paul," Casey said, "I know you have to work these things out during your business hours, but if you go to see Mrs. Dittman, and it's after school, could Alison and I go with you?"

Paul looked at his watch. "Tell you what, Casey. Why don't I see if I can get in touch with Mrs. Dittman right now? We'll see what we can do."

He got up to use the phone, and Casey tried to keep calm and sit still until he came back. It seemed to take an awfully long time. She wanted so much to go. She hoped Mrs. Dittman's answer would be yes.

"It's okay," Paul said, coming back into the room. "She's on our side all the way. She said her husband is out of town, and we can all come over. Gladys will meet us there. Now, if you ask your mother . . ."

"Ask your mother what?" Mrs. Cooper came through the doorway, rubbing her fingers. "It's nice to see you, Paul. I didn't know you were here. I thought it was a friend of Casey's."

"I am a friend of Casey's," he said, and they all laughed. "Will you give her permission to come with me to interview Harvey Atterbury's daughter?"

"Oh, Casey, you're going to keep on with this?" her mother asked.

"We had a terrific response to the story," Paul said.

"We're going to do a follow-up, and Casey wants to be there."

"And Alison too," Casey said. "If you say I can go, Mom, I'll call Alison."

"You may go with Paul," her mother said, and Casey raced to the phone to call her friend.

Alison was wearing the sweater she got for her birthday and a new pair of slacks when they picked her up.

"You didn't have to get all dressed up," Casey complained, rubbing her hands down the legs of her jeans.

"Just in case," Alison said, giving Casey a knowing look.

But Casey's mind was on meeting Lydia Dittman. "What's she going to be like?" she asked Paul.

"She sounded very friendly," Paul said.

And she was. She invited the three of them into her large home which rested in the middle of a ridge in Hollywood Hills, with a view of the city of Los Angeles from her front windows and a view of a pool and rose garden from the side.

She handed them soft drinks and gracefully seated herself on a circular sofa that stretched in front of the fireplace like a comfortable cat. She brushed back her shining brown hair.

"I watched your television program," she said. "I think you girls have a fine idea." She took a sip of her drink and added, "I remember Rosalie from when I was a little girl. She's a delightful person."

"Do you think you could talk your husband into giving her a job?" Casey asked.

"No, I don't," she said. She gave a little laugh. "Don't look so discouraged, Casey. I've come up with an alternate idea. I'll tell you about it, and you can give me your opinion."

Casey nodded vigorously and shifted in her chair. She quickly picked up the ashtray her knees had nudged off the coffee table. Luckily it wasn't broken. "I'm all for anything that will help Rosalie," she said.

"We have a charter flight about once a month into Tijuana," Lydia said. "You know where Tijuana is?"

"Right across the border in Mexico," Alison answered.

"There are no scheduled flights on United States carriers into the Tijuana airport, but charter flights are allowed; so we have a flight that goes down there and back in one day. One is scheduled for Saturday. Do you think Rosalie would like to wear an Atterbury uniform and serve as an attendant on that flight?"

"Just the one?" Casey asked.

"It's a beginning. If your television news director is willing," she said to Paul, "you could cover the flight with your cameraman."

"Camera person," Casey said.

Lydia smiled and continued. "It might give Rosalie the extra publicity she'd need. If Atterbury Airlines

90

won't offer her a job, then perhaps some other airline will."

Casey clapped her hands together. "Terrific!" she shouted. "It's a great idea! Isn't it, Paul?"

"I like it," he said. "I don't think I'll have any trouble selling the idea to our news director—not after the response we got from the interview with Rosalie."

"Fine," Lydia said. "The flight isn't full. I checked. I'll reserve four seats for the three of you and your camera—person—in other names."

"For us?" Alison gasped.

"You mean Alison and I can go too?" Casey said.

"Of course you can go," Lydia told them. "It wouldn't be as good a story if you weren't there."

Casey realized all that Lydia had said. "Why do we have to use other names?"

"It's just a precaution," Lydia said. "I'd rather that Rodney and my father didn't find out about our plan in advance."

"They might stop us?"

"Let's not give them the chance," Lydia said. "Now—for Rosalie's uniform. Let me know what size she wears, and I'll have one ready for her."

The doorbell rang, and Lydia jumped.

"It's probably Gladys, our photographer," Paul said. He went to the door with Lydia.

"I wonder what scared her," Casey said.

"She just wasn't expecting the doorbell to ring," Alison said.

"Do you jump every time the doorbell rings?"

"Well . . . no," Alison said.

Lydia Dittman came back into the room, with Paul and Gladys behind her. "Remember," she said to all of them, "this plan for Saturday is our secret. When you interview me now, we'll just talk about Rosalie and Atterbury Airlines and my position on the board of directors without any real power to it . . . certainly not enough power to hire Rosalie Mertz."

Her glance at Casey and Alison was firm and intense as she said, "I don't want anyone to know about our plans for Saturday's flight to Tijuana! Not anyone!"

11   The Second Warning!

The interview with Lydia Dittman was on the news the next day.

Casey's mother sighed when it was over and said, "I just hope we've made the right decision about letting you go on that flight. You're so young to be traveling alone."

"She won't be alone," Mr. Cooper said. He shook the can of salted nuts he'd been munching from to see if there were any left in the bottom. "Casey will be with her Siamese twin, an aging airline stewardess, a television reporter and a photographer—just your average group of incognito traveling companions."

Casey laughed. "Mom, you talked to Rosalie. She

said she'd take very good care of us. It's just for one day." She jumped up and turned off the television. "Paul's going to take our pictures while we're in Tijuana, too! We're going to have so much fun! Alison and I have never been to Mexico!"

The phone rang, and she raced for it, yelling, "That's Alison!"

But the voice was the same disguised deep voice she had heard before. "I warned you," he said.

Casey wasn't as frightened this time as she had been when she first heard the voice. "Who are you?" she demanded. "What right have you got to try to scare me?"

"Back off, little girl," he said. "Go find something else to do, or you'll be sorry."

Casey felt shivery, but she held her ground. "You listen to me!" she began. There was a sharp click in her ear, and she realized the person had hung up. Slowly she put down the receiver. Who was this person? Why didn't he want her to help Rosalie get her job back? That must be his problem, not Sylvia's arrest.

"Who was that, dear?" her mother asked, as she came into the kitchen, carrying the dirty glasses and empty salted-nut can. In a moment they had disappeared into their proper places, and the sink and counter had been wiped clean.

"It was just someone who saw the television news," Casey said. She tried to change the subject quickly.

"Did I tell you about the report I gave in school yesterday? I got another A."

"Wonderful!" her mother said, hugging her.

Casey gave her mother a quick kiss on the cheek and pulled away. "I'd better get ready for bed now," she said. She didn't want to take the chance that her mother would ask any more questions about the telephone call.

Casey had no sooner reached the door to her room when the doorbell rang. She jumped, and remembered the way Lydia Dittman had been startled, too, when her doorbell rang. What was Casey expecting? What had Lydia been expecting? Casey was almost afraid to find out.

She heard her father open the door and give an exclamation of surprise. Curiosity led her back down the hallway to join her father.

"There's no one here," he said.

Her mother came to her side, wiping her hands on a dish towel. "Who is it?"

"No one," Mr. Cooper said.

Casey felt the shivers begin again and travel up and down her backbone like little electric shocks.

"What is that?" Mrs. Cooper asked.

"Don't go out there!" Casey gasped.

"Nonsense," her father said. "We have to find out what is going on."

Casey came to the doorway as her father stepped

into the small circle of light from the porch lamp. He bent over, reached out, and grabbed something.

"I don't believe it!" he shouted. "Look at this!"

Casey stumbled over the doormat and clutched her mother's arm.

"My old fishing hat!" Mr. Cooper said. "It's on top of this pile of stuff. Look! A couple of old shirts, a broken vase, a . . . What in the world is this? It looks like a rusty corn-bread pan!"

"The garage sale," Casey managed to say. "The last customer took all the stuff that was left. I guess he didn't want it and brought it back!"

"He dumped it right on our doormat!" Mrs. Cooper gasped. "What a terrible thing to do!"

"It's not terrible," Mr. Cooper said. "That guy is one in a million! Imagine, he brought back my fishing hat! He ought to get a reward!"

Casey helped her parents carry the assortment of odds and ends to the trash can. She was glad the plaster elephant ashtray and the picture of an erupting volcano in a seashell frame weren't in the pile. And she giggled with relief when she thought how scared she had been for nothing.

She refused to be afraid anymore. What had Paul said about the TV station always getting a few crank calls? Well, that's what she had got—a crank call from some kind of a crank, and she wasn't going to worry about it.

It was hard to wait until Saturday. Casey didn't need the alarm clock to wake up. She was dressed in a plaid jumper and white blouse that her mother had chosen, and was seated at the kitchen table, munching her way through a piece of toast, before the sky had begun to lighten.

Her father came into the kitchen in his pajamas, rubbing his head. "What time is it?" he asked.

"Almost time for Paul to come by," she answered.

"Why would anyone want to take a flight this early in the morning?"

Casey threw her arms around her father's neck and hugged him, accidentally dropping a chunk of toast down the back of his pajama top.

"Hey," he said, backing away. "Wait until I can wake up enough to defend myself."

Everything seemed to happen in a hurry. Paul and Gladys arrived, Casey kissed her parents good-bye and was bundled into the back seat of Paul's car. Alison and Rosalie were picked up, Rosalie looking magnificent in her stewardess uniform, and they headed for the small airport in the San Fernando Valley.

"We're to meet Mrs. Dittman in the Atterbury Airlines office at the airport," Paul said, as he drove into the parking lot.

"I thought we'd be going to the International Airport," Alison said.

"No. Many charter flights use the smaller airports around Los Angeles," Rosalie said. Her eyes gleamed. "This is like old times!"

Rosalie led the way as they bustled into the Atterbury Airlines office with its dull green walls and plastic chairs. Lydia seemed to appear out of nowhere and went through the door with them.

"Rodney," she said. "Here are some passengers for you." Casey noticed that Lydia's hands were trembling.

A man standing behind a desk whirled and stared at them. A woman in a flight attendant uniform, who had been talking to him, let her mouth fall open in surprise.

"What's this all about?" he asked. He pointed at Rosalie. "And what's she doing in one of our uniforms?"

Lydia ignored his questions and smiled at Casey's group. "This is my husband, Rodney Dittman, president of Atterbury Airlines, and one of our flight attendants, Annabelle McFarland."

They all spoke at once, acknowledging the introductions. Paul stepped forward and held out his hand.

Rodney scowled and made no attempt to shake hands. "You didn't answer my question, Lydia. I recognize these people from the Channel 12 News. And I demand to know, why is this woman wearing one of our uniforms?"

"Rosalie Mertz is wearing a uniform because I gave it to her," Lydia said. "She's going to serve as one of the flight attendants on this charter flight to Tijuana."

Miss McFarland's eyes grew panicky, and she stared at Rodney. "She can't do that," she said. "Anyhow, the flight is filled. We haven't seats for these people."

"Oh yes we have," Lydia said. She waved a fistful of tickets. "I've got tickets for all of them."

Rodney looked as though he couldn't believe what was happening. "Lydia," he said, "why are you doing this?"

"Because I think it's a good idea," she said. "You never have liked any of my ideas for promoting the airline, and I think I've had some good ones. I suddenly realized, as I saw Rosalie being interviewed on the news program, that I *am* a member of the board, and it's about time I exercised some of the rights that go with that position."

"But what's the reason?" Rodney leaned on the desk and glowered at her from under his ledge of eyebrows.

"The reason is this. I think Rosalie deserves a job as a flight attendant. She has an excellent record. She's in good health. If she flies with Atterbury Airlines on this trip, the story might give her the publicity she needs to get a job again. If you won't budge, maybe some other airline will."

She smiled at him. "The publicity won't hurt Atterbury Airlines either."

"We don't want publicity!" he began, but he suddenly stopped talking.

Casey looked at Miss McFarland and had the weird feeling that she had given him some kind of signal to keep quiet. Casey gave a little shake of her head. She was letting her imagination run away with her.

Annabelle McFarland stepped forward. She wore a professional smile, but her eyes were like cold marbles. "Mrs. Dittman," she said, "I'm in charge of this flight, and I'll be glad to find a job for Mrs. Mertz to do. Of course, she'll be unfamiliar with modern service."

Rosalie interrupted. "Oh, I've flown enough, visiting my children back East, to keep up with what is going on. I'll be a hard worker, I promise."

Miss McFarland's penciled-on smile didn't change. There was something wrong here, Casey thought. Did Mrs. Dittman know what it was? Casey studied her face. She didn't think so. Lydia Dittman had the expression of someone who had taken a brave stand for what she thought was right and was feeling good about it.

Other passengers were beginning to arrive. A man in an Atterbury Airlines uniform entered the room and stepped behind a counter. Automatically, all the passengers formed a line, presented their tickets to him, and received boarding passes with seat selection.

"Non-smoking section, please," Casey said as she and Alison moved to the counter. "And could we have window seats?"

"Just one window seat left," he said. "Who shall I give it to?"

"To Alison," Casey said quickly. She had the feeling that there were going to be things to watch on the plane as well as outside the plane. She was aware that Rodney had moved to stand by one of the large plate glass windows and seemed to be very anxious about what might be outside. Miss McFarland had left the room. Casey didn't know where she had gone.

"Anytime you want to look out the window, I'll trade places with you," Alison was saying. Casey mumbled something in return.

"One window seat and one aisle," the attendant said, handing them their tickets and boarding passes.

Alison grabbed Casey's arm. "Casey! We'll be taking off in just fifteen minutes! Aren't you excited?"

"You know it," Casey answered. She wasn't about to tell Alison that there was something else she was feeling besides excitement.

Maybe it was the warnings she had received over the telephone.

Maybe it was the strange way in which Rodney Dittman and Annabelle McFarland had acted.

Down in the pit of Casey's stomach was a small, growing knot of fear!

12 | Up Against a Block

The plane wasn't as large as the one Casey had flown when her family took a vacation trip to Washington, D.C. There were only two seats on each side of the aisle, and she guessed that the plane held only about eighty passengers. There was no division between first-class and coach sections. All the passengers were flying on the same priced tickets, so Casey, from her seat near the back of the plane, could get a good look at most of the people on the plane.

Miss McFarland had assigned Rosalie to assist the people in the back of the plane. She took the front section, and a flight attendant named Judy was stationed in the center.

Casey looked at her watch. It was time they took off,

but the door at the front of the plane remained open.

"Look, Casey. Those women almost missed the plane," Alison said, glancing out the window.

Casey leaned across her to see. Two young women, carrying babies bundled up in layers of blankets, were walking as fast as they could toward the steps of the plane.

"Why would they want to take their babies to Tijuana for a day?" Casey asked Alison.

"Who cares?" Alison said. "We're going to take off soon!"

Casey watched the door of the plane, but as the women came on board, Miss McFarland blocked Casey's line of vision. She bustled around the women, helping them into the first two seats on the left side of the plane. Since Casey and Alison were also on the left side, that was the last look Casey was able to get of the women and babies.

The door was swung closed and locked, and the sound from the plane's jet engines increased. Slowly, they began to move, then headed out toward the runway. "I love takeoffs!" Alison said with a frozen smile. She gripped Casey's arm so tightly it hurt.

"Take it easy. We're not leaving yet," she managed to answer. Annabelle McFarland was demonstrating the use of oxygen masks, in case of emergency, and Casey wanted to pay attention.

Paul, across the aisle, reached over and patted Ca-

sey's hand. Casey realized she was gripping the arms of the seat as tightly as Alison was holding her arm.

"Ready, set, go . . ." Paul said. The plane picked up speed, and suddenly Casey realized they were off the ground and climbing high in the sky. She swallowed a few times to break the pressure in her eardrums.

In a surprisingly short while, the captain introduced himself over the loudspeaker and informed the passengers they could unfasten their seat belts if they wished.

"Whew!" Alison relaxed. But Paul and Gladys were in the aisle, Gladys taking films of Rosalie, who was pushing the cart of drinks into the aisle from the galley in the rear of the plane.

Annabelle McFarland put out a hand and stopped the cart. "Judy and I will take it from here," she said. "When it reaches the midpoint coming back, you and Judy can finish."

It made sense to Casey. Yet, in another way, it didn't make sense. Annabelle was making sure Rosalie didn't get to the front of the plane. If Rosalie couldn't, then maybe Casey could.

She stood up. "Want to stretch your legs?" she asked Alison.

"On the ground," Alison said. "You aren't going to walk very far in this plane, Casey."

"I'm going to walk up to the front of the plane and back again."

"You're going to walk only as far as that cart in the aisle and back again," Alison said. "You can't squeeze around that cart."

Casey shrugged, defeated. Alison was right.

Rosalie was having a wonderful time, and Casey thought that the passengers in Rosalie's section were lucky. Somehow Rosalie managed to prepare some hot milk for a man who had a headache, and she rubbed his neck until he smiled and said he felt one hundred percent better. A woman with too much makeup and gigantic sunglasses held Rosalie's hand and told her all about her divorce, while Rosalie clucked sympathetically. And a woman who said she had three teen-agers and was going bananas listened eagerly to Rosalie's advice, while she nodded her head up and down in agreement as fast as a bird going for bread crumbs.

Rosalie stopped by Casey's seat as the cart came down the aisle close to her. "I love what I'm doing," she said to Casey.

Casey pulled her down to whisper into her ear. "Rosalie, is Annabelle McFarland keeping you from going to the front of the plane?"

"No," Rosalie said. She looked surprised.

"Could you go up there if you wanted to?"

"I'm sure I could."

"Then, Rosalie, please do something for me." Casey made her voice even lower. "Take a look at those women with the babies. Something is wrong about them. I know it is."

Rosalie stood up slowly and looked down the aisle. There was a question in her eyes, but she shrugged and nodded at Casey.

She began to move around to the other side of the cart, but Judy put a hand on her arm. "No, Rosalie. I'll take that side. You work this one."

"I just thought . . ." Rosalie began, but Judy had maneuvered the cart to block Rosalie's way, and had already squeezed around it.

Rosalie gave Casey a knowing look, and Casey was satisfied that Rosalie also sensed something was wrong. What it was, Casey was bound and determined to find out.

Casey drank her soft drink, munched her packet of salted peanuts and made plans for when they left the plane. It wouldn't take long to get to Tijuana, and she was going to be ready when they landed, to get a good look at the two women in the front of the plane.

But when they landed, and the plane had rolled to a stop, everyone stood up to collect their things, and Judy was in the aisle in front of Casey.

"Excuse me, please," Casey said, trying to edge past the flight attendant.

"Just a minute," Judy said, giving Casey a look as though her rudeness was inexcusable. "There are people ahead of you."

"There's someone up there I have to see," Casey said.

"You'll just have to wait," Judy told her.

Some of the people in the aisle ahead of Casey were staring at her. Casey took a look at the array of large handbags and sweaters and plump men and hippy women she would have to push her way through. She slumped. There was no way she could make it.

"We'll be going through customs, Casey," Paul said. "You don't need to be in such a hurry. You'll only have to get in a line and wait in customs."

"Isn't customs for people who are buying things?" Alison asked.

"It's a checkpoint as you go into any country, where officials can make sure that nothing is being brought into their country that shouldn't be. You'll go through customs inspection when we get back to Los Angeles, too."

"Good," Casey said. She looked back and saw Rosalie helping a woman on with her jacket. Rosalie was still at the back of the plane. "We'll have a chance to get a good look at those women," she whispered to Alison.

"What women?" Alison whispered back.

"The ones up ahead with the babies."

But before she could leave the plane, Annabelle McFarland stepped into her path and put a firm hand on her shoulder. "I don't think you want to get off the

plane yet, Casey. I'm sure that Mr. Baker will want his photographer to get some shots of all of you leaving the plane, and Rosalie helping you with your things."

"He has plenty of shots of Rosalie," Casey began, but Annabelle continued, smiling up at Paul.

"You might want some pictures of us with Rosalie and the girls," she said. Her mouth puckered into a little pout. "Judy and I feel left out of all the excitement. We'd love to see ourselves on television, too."

"Of course you will," Paul said. "I wouldn't neglect you."

"I'll just go ahead to the customs room and wait for you there," Casey told him.

Paul shook his head. "I'm responsible for you," he said. "I want you under my thumb."

"But, Paul," she complained.

"Be patient, Casey," he said. "We've got a whole day to spend in Tijuana. There's lots of time."

He didn't understand, Casey thought. There wasn't enough time. She was going to miss getting a close look at those women with the babies, and for some reason she felt there was something about those women that was very important to find out!

13 | Casey, the Detective

It was just as Casey thought. When they finally got to the room where the customs inspection was held, most of the passengers had left. Casey was sure that Annabelle and Judy had been stalling them deliberately. She put her straw handbag on the counter and watched the customs official poke through it halfheartedly.

"Okay," he said, waving her on through the passway toward the airport waiting room.

"Can you tell me about two women who came through here—women carrying babies?" she asked him.

He looked surprised. "No, *señorita*. I didn't see any women carrying babies."

113

"But they were on the plane. They got off first, and . . ."

He interrupted, pushing back his hat and scratching the red mark it left around his forehead. "There were many people here at once," he said. "Maybe the women you speak of went through one of the other stations."

Casey looked around. "There aren't any other of-ficials here."

"They left after most of the passengers had gone through," he said turning to Alison, showing Casey he was through with the conversation.

"Come on, Casey," Alison said, pushing her through the passway. "We're going to have a whole day of fun in Mexico! Forget about those women and their babies!"

Rosalie, Paul and Gladys soon joined them. Casey watched Annabelle and Judy and the pilot and co-pilot go out a side door in the small airport waiting room. "They are up to something," she said.

"What are you talking about?" Paul asked.

"I don't know."

Paul laughed. "Then forget about it. We're off to Tijuana to get a good feature story."

"And have fun!" Alison added.

They did. Gladys shot some film of them browsing through the shops and stalls along the main tourist streets in the border town. Some of the stores were

114

large, with carts and checkout stands; but Casey's favorites were the small, dusty shops with piles of baskets and hand-painted clay bean pots and bright *piñatas*. Alison picked out a straw horse, and Casey bought a copper bracelet and a T-shirt with *¡Liberacion!* printed on it.

A clerk showed Casey and Alison how to twirl a *molinillo* between their hands to beat the chocolate drink to foam, and Paul led the way to the Fronton Palacio where the jai alai games were held.

They stopped for lunch in a large, very pretty restaurant decorated with potted plants and birds in cages. Casey concentrated so hard on seating herself gracefully that she tripped over a chair leg, banged her knee into a table leg, and sent a filled water glass tumbling to the floor.

"Oh, no!" she groaned, as two waiters came hurrying, and people began looking up to see who was causing a problem.

Casey mumbled apologies to anyone who would listen. She stood back, out of the way of the waiters, and happened to glance across the room. A couple was leaving a table, their lunches hardly touched, and moving rapidly toward the far door. As they went through the door Casey caught a glimpse of the woman's face and gasped.

"What's the matter?" Rosalie asked her.

"The woman who just left," Casey said. "I think she

was one of the women on the plane—one of the women carrying babies."

"There's nothing strange about that."

"But she didn't have her baby with her."

Rosalie's forehead puckered as she thought. "There's always a logical explanation for everything, Casey. Perhaps the other woman is taking care of both babies for a little while."

"Maybe," Casey said. The waiters had finished re-setting the table, and stood back as Casey very carefully seated herself. They let out a sigh of relief as she managed to do so without any more upsets. One of them handed out menus, and the other scurried off.

Casey said to Rosalie, "But do me a favor, please? When we're back at the plane, will you try to get a good look at those women? Maybe you'll be able to discover what it is that's making me feel something is not just right."

Rosalie nodded. "Consider it done," she said.

Casey added, under her breath, "If Annabelle and Judy won't get in the way."

After lunch there was more time for shopping, and Casey was surprised when Paul said it was time to get to the airport. They found a cab and all of them piled in, squeezed together with their straw animals, pottery jars and Rosalie's hand-tooled leather bag.

Casey closed her eyes. The ride was fast and bumpy, and she was sure they were going to hit another car. She didn't open her eyes until they reached the airport, and the taxi stopped with a squeal of brakes.

They presented their tickets, and boarding time was called.

"The women with the babies aren't here," Casey told Alison, taking her aside.

"They were late before," Alison said. "Why are you so worried about them?"

"Because I don't trust them," Casey said.

"What could they be doing wrong?" Alison asked. "You aren't going to suspect nice young mothers with sweet little babies of doing something awful like smuggling, are you?"

"Smuggling?" Casey stared at Alison. Things began falling into place.

"You know," Alison explained. "It's one of the reasons we have to go through customs."

Casey smiled and grabbed Alison's arms. "That's it! Of course! What a great way to smuggle something— inside a baby's blankets! Alison, I think we've got it!"

"Casey, you don't have proof of anything," Alison said. "You can't accuse those women of smuggling."

"It's just a suspicion right now," Casey said, "but I'm going to find out the truth. Look, Alison, I got some warning phone calls, telling me to mind my own business."

"You didn't tell me that!" Alison squealed.

"Keep your voice down," Casey said. "I just thought the phone calls were from some kind of a crank. I didn't want to worry you about them. But think about Mr. Dittman, too. He didn't want us to go on this flight. And Annabelle and Judy are keeping all of us—including Rosalie—at the back of the plane, away from those women."

"Shouldn't you tell Rosalie or Paul about this?"

"I'm going to tell Rosalie right now. We'll need her help to find out. They won't let us get anywhere near those babies."

But Casey was surprised. As they walked to the stairs that led to the door of the plane, the two women came hurrying through the small waiting room and joined them.

Casey hung back. She peered down into the first blanket and saw two blue eyes peering back at her. "That's a darling baby," she said to the woman carrying the child.

"Thanks," the woman said abruptly. "Hurry up. They're waiting for us."

As they stepped into the plane, Casey passed the three flight attendants, who were smiling at them. She threw a puzzled look at Rosalie, who simply shrugged. The other two hadn't allowed Rosalie in the front of the plane on the flight to Tijuana. Now, they didn't seem to care where she was.

The routine began. Annabelle and Judy were busy

helping people stow their purchases in the various compartments inside the plane. Everyone was seated in the same seats they had been assigned on the flight down, and Rosalie made sure all seat belts were fastened and seats were upright for takeoff. Finally, Annabelle gave her brief lecture, reminding the passengers of safety regulations.

The plane taxied out on the runway and took off. Casey managed to break Alison's grip on her arm. Both babies began to wail.

Rosalie walked briskly up the aisle, and Casey grabbed her skirt. "Rosalie," she said, "why are the babies crying?"

"It's the pressure on the ears when we take off and land," Rosalie said. "You're old enough to swallow or yawn to break the pressure. Poor little babies don't know what to do. For a few minutes it hurts them."

She went down the aisle, Paul and Gladys following. Casey saw her bend over the two women with babies. In just a moment the crying stopped. A thought tickled the back of Casey's mind, but refused to come forward. There was something she should be remembering.

Casey was surprised to see Annabelle and Judy working to get the cart up the aisle. They didn't seem the least concerned about keeping Rosalie in the back of the plane. Casey wondered if they would feel the same way about her.

She stood up and moved into the aisle. "Excuse me," she said to Judy, "May I please get by?"

She was surprised when Judy stepped aside and said, "Just squeeze past."

Casey did and went up the aisle to join Rosalie, who was on her way back.

"Did you notice anything unusual about the women with the babies?" Casey whispered.

"I didn't pay much attention to the women, just to the babies," Rosalie answered. "Poor little things. They've got too many blankets around them. Those women aren't very wise mothers, or they'd know you don't have to bundle a baby up like that."

Casey hurried back to Alison and squeezed her hand. "Something is being smuggled! I'm sure of it!" She kept her voice low. "Alison! Because we don't have any proof yet, you and I are the only ones who can do anything to stop it!"

14 | Call the Police!

"What do you want us to do?" Alison asked. "Casey, we could get into a lot of trouble!" She took a second look at her friend and moaned. "Oh, Casey, I should have known that anything you'd get mixed up in would . . ."

"Listen to me, Alison," Casey interrupted. "I need your help."

"You don't need me," Alison said. "You need the police. You need the customs inspectors. You need . . ."

"That's right, and that's why I need you. I don't have any proof, and I can't inspect those baby blankets myself. So you're going to have to make sure you're the first person off the plane. You go right to one of the customs inspectors and tell him we think the women are smuggling something."

"I don't like the idea." Alison slumped in her seat and looked at Casey with despair.

"I need you, Alison," Casey said. "Do this for me, and I'll . . . well, I'll try to think up a way for you to meet Randolph Mantooth."

"Casey! If you ruin anything between Randolph Mantooth and me . . ."

"There isn't anything between you and Randolph Mantooth," Casey said. "It's got to be started before it can be ruined."

"You really think you could come up with a way I could meet him?"

"I told you, I promise to work on the idea. Will you tell the customs inspector?"

"Okay," Alison said. "Just this one time, Casey. But after this, if you're wrong, I'll never help you with one of your ideas again!"

"Thanks, Alison," Casey said, patting her friend's arm. "I knew I could count on you." She leaned over Alison to look out the window. "I bet we'll be landing pretty soon."

In just a few minutes an announcement was made that they were slowly descending and approaching the San Fernando Valley Airport. Casey gulped to make her ears pop. The babies began their pitiful little cries again, and Casey felt sorry for them.

The wheels of the plane lowered with a final thump, and soon the plane was on the ground, bumping and braking and decreasing its speed.

Casey unfastened Alison's seat belt and pulled her over on her lap. She squeezed out from under and got in Alison's seat.

"Casey, I think this is illegal!" Alison said. "The seat-belt sign is still on!"

"Don't worry," Casey whispered. "The minute the plane stops you have to get up the aisle as fast as you can!"

"But my straw horse!"

"I'll take care of all that. Ready . . . get ready. . . . Go, Alison!"

The plane gave its final lurch as it came to a complete stop. Alison stumbled down the aisle, managing to wiggle and squeeze between the few passengers who were climbing into the aisle. Casey could see the stairs being rolled against the side of the plane. Finally, the big door was opened. She watched Alison run down the stairs, as though she were after a ribbon in the relays, and dash toward the customs room in the airport.

Casey couldn't see what Annabelle and Judy were doing. There were too many people in the way. She hung back, waiting at the end of the line to collect Alison's straw horse and her paper bag of souvenirs from the large compartment at the front of the plane where Annabelle had stored them. She wanted to keep an eye on those two flight attendants. If there was some smuggling going on, they were definitely in on it.

Most of the people were off the plane. The women with the babies had probably been among the first, as they had been in Tijuana, with their crying babies and . . .

Casey held her breath as the thought struck her.

"Isn't this yours?" A voice broke into her thoughts, and she found herself staring open-mouthed at Annabelle. The woman held a package toward Casey. "I said, isn't this yours?"

"Oh, yes, thank you," Casey said. "And that straw horse. That's my friend's." She tried to peer into the compartment. "And that big box in the back. That's hers too."

"No, it isn't," Annabelle said. She carefully shut the door of the compartment.

Rosalie stepped up. "It might be Alison's," she said. "Goodness knows we brought enough souvenirs to fill a taxicab!"

Annabelle stood with her back to the compartment door. "No," she said smoothly. "That box belongs to me." She nodded toward Paul, who was waiting in the doorway. "I think your TV people want more film, Rosalie. It looks as though this is the end of your last trip as a flight attendant."

Now Casey was sure—well, pretty sure.

"Paul . . . Rosalie," she said breathlessly. "I think we'd better get to the customs office as fast as we can!"

She raced down the stairs, not waiting for the others, and ran into the small building. Alison was standing there, clutching the back of a chair, looking as though she had been betrayed.

"Where were you, Casey?" she cried.

The two customs officials had the babies on the table, blankets and clothing aside. Both babies lay there kicking happily in nothing but their diapers, and both women were angrily talking at once, wanting to know just what the inspectors thought they were doing.

One of the officials scowled at Casey, as she pushed her way to his station. "Are you the one who insisted these women were smuggling something in the babies' clothing?"

"No," Casey said. "I just asked Alison to tell you these women were smuggling something." She was aware that Paul and Rosalie had come up behind her and that Gladys had moved beside the station, lights on, camera going.

"But we've examined their handbags. We've examined the baby clothes and blankets. We can't find anything," the official said.

"That's because you're looking for the wrong thing," Casey said. "What's being smuggled is right under your noses! The babies!"

"Babies?" Everyone in earshot turned and stared at her.

"Yes," Casey said. "On the trip down to Tijuana the flight attendants wouldn't let us get near the women with the babies, and they were the last on the plane. Coming back to Los Angeles no one seemed to care how many of us got a good look at the babies. But most important, I remembered that on the trip down the babies didn't cry when the pressure changed in the plane. On the way back they did! Don't you see?"

One of the officials moved toward the two women, blocking their way from the room. "Tell us the rest," he said.

"They aren't smuggling something *with* the babies," Casey said. "They're smuggling the babies themselves! On the plane, in the large compartment near the front, is a big box. Inside it I think you'll find some life-size baby dolls wrapped in identical blankets."

"But why?" Alison's voice broke the moment of stunned silence. "Why would anyone smuggle babies?"

One of the women began to cry. "It wasn't so bad!" she said. "There are lots of people in the United States who want to adopt babies and can't because there aren't enough. And there are people in other countries who are willing to supply babies if the price is right. Papers are easy to forge."

128

"Selling babies!" a man shouted. "That's terrible!"

Then everyone began shouting at once. Casey could hear Rosalie yelling, "Where's a telephone? We have to call the police!"

The police came too soon. Casey couldn't believe it. As though by magic, the door to the airport waiting room flew open and policemen hurried in. Casey was pushed this way and that, and she was doubly surprised to see that Sylvia Schweppe was with them! Somebody stepped on her foot, the corner of someone else's leather handbag poked her in the ear, and she almost lost her grip on Alison's straw horse. The door to the runway opened, and even more policemen came in with the plane crew.

One of the men with Sylvia looked as though he were in charge. "Quiet, please!" he shouted, until the hubbub in the room stopped, and everyone stood still and listened.

"May I have your attention, please," he said. Only the buzz of Gladys' camera could be heard.

"Oh, Mac!" Sylvia said. "I know you're going to be awful mad, but they said I'd get a much lighter sentence if I told them all about you and how to find you."

"Shut up!" Annabelle McFarland snapped.

Casey said aloud, "Mac? Annabelle McFarland? Was she the one who planned the bank robbery? Is she the one who worked out this baby smuggling?"

No one answered her, but no one needed to.

Sylvia and the crew and the policemen disappeared through the outer door like water going down the drain. As the co-pilot passed Casey, he growled under his breath, "I told you to mind your own business, kid!" This was the voice she had heard on the phone, but it didn't bother Casey now.

The customs inspectors hurried people through the passways, and Alison hugged Casey. "Tomorrow! No later than tomorrow! You've got to come up with the idea of how I can meet Randolph Mantooth!"

"And so," Paul was saying into his microphone, "this is Paul Baker with another on-the-spot story from Channel 12 News, Los Angeles!"

15 | Just One More Good Idea

Casey didn't stop talking until the late newscast began. There was so much to tell her parents and Eugenia. The newscast was exciting because Gladys had covered everything, even some shots of one of the women trying to get away, which Casey had missed. Somehow Casey found herself tucked into bed. Her last thought was that she'd never possibly be able to fall asleep.

When the sun woke her in the morning, she wasn't too sure that she hadn't dreamed the whole thing. But her mother greeted Casey as she started to the breakfast table, sleepily struggling into her robe, and said, "Look who's here!"

Rosalie laughed, and put down her coffee cup. "I

had to tell you my news in person, Casey. Even though it's Sunday, I've been on the phone all morning."

Casey slipped into the nearest chair. "What news?" she asked. Suddenly she was wide-awake.

"I've had a job offer from one of the major airlines. They want me to start a Grandmother Service complete with hot cocoa and animal crackers. The vice-president who called me was excited. He thinks they'd get ahead of their competitors with grandmother-attendants on longer flights."

Casey jumped up and down in her chair. "Fantastic!" she shouted.

"Just think," Rosalie said. "I'd be traveling all over the United States. Maybe to Europe or South America. I know it's what you'd want me to do."

Casey stopped bouncing. She looked carefully at Rosalie. "What *I'd* want you to do? Why do you say that?"

"Well," Rosalie said, "you have managed things so far, Casey—and very nicely, I might add."

Casey thought a moment. "Let's not talk about what you think I want. What do *you* want to do, Rosalie?"

Rosalie smiled. "It seems that Rodney Dittman was a part of that baby-smuggling ring, and Harvey Atterbury is going to need someone else to run his airline. He finally admitted to his daughter, after she kept him up arguing all night long, that she's got what it takes to build Atterbury Airlines into a really successful airline. So she phoned me. She wants me to help her organize a really super flight attendant service."

"But you wouldn't get to fly."

"Oh yes I would—once in a while. She said if I got lonesome for my old job I could take that Los Angeles—Tijuana charter run any time I wanted."

"Do you know what I think you should do?" Casey asked. "I think you should take the job you'd like the best, and not do what you think someone else would want you to do."

"That's good advice," her mother said.

"Then it's Atterbury Airlines," Rosalie said. "I've got real loyalties there, Casey."

"Who knows? It might even lead to romance between you and your old friend Harvey Atterbury," Mrs. Cooper said.

"Never in a million years!" Rosalie said, draining the coffee from her cup. She stood up. "Now since that's settled, I'll get home and call Lydia and tell her I'm ready to go to work."

"I'm glad, Rosalie," Casey said.

"And I'm glad you got me into all this," Rosalie answered. "I like your ideas on equal rights for women in the job market. Look what they did for me!"

After Rosalie left, Mrs. Cooper handed her daughter a plate of cinnamon rolls.

"I'm too excited to eat," Casey said.

Her mother sat beside her. "I think you gave Rosalie the right answer. You left the choice up to her. You felt she should do what she wants to do."

"I guess that's a part of equal rights," Casey said, "the right to make a choice."

"Yes," her mother answered. "The right to work at a job outside the home, or within the home."

Casey sat upright and blinked. "Are you telling me you want to cop out on your typing lessons and getting a job to fulfill yourself, Mom?"

"There's no copping out involved, Casey. It's still a matter of choice. Some people love working in an office. But there are some people who love working in a home. I'm sure there are men who would rather work in a home, if they had a choice."

"What a good idea," Casey said. "I wonder if Daddy . . ."

Her mother smiled. "Why don't you ask him instead of making up your own answer?"

"I get the message," Casey said. "I haven't been giving you your right to make a choice. I've been interfering with you."

"Not interfering, you were trying to help."

"Mom," Casey said, "I promise I won't interfere with anyone ever again."

"Not even Eugenia and Paul?"

"What about Eugenia and Paul?" Casey got to her feet.

"They're coming over to dinner today," Mrs. Cooper said. "They'll be here in a little while. I just have a hunch, Casey, that . . ."

"Oh, no, Mom! Eugenia has a career! She wouldn't want to get married!"

"She's free to make choices, isn't she? There's no reason why she can't choose to do both."

The front door opened, and Eugenia and Paul came in, laughing and chattering. They made their way to the kitchen, and Eugenia called out, "There she is! There's the celebrity! Have you seen the morning newspapers, Casey?"

Eugenia looked awfully happy, and so did Paul. Casey took a deep breath and found she really didn't mind at all if they decided they wanted to fall in love and get married. Paul was a nice guy, and people did fall in love. Even Alison, who . . .

"Paul, I just thought of something," Casey said. "You work in television. Is there any chance that you might someday meet Randolph Mantooth?"

"Sure," Paul said. "I happen to know Randolph Mantooth. He went to school with my brother. What's this about Randolph Mantooth?"

Casey grinned. "Oh, Paul!" she said. "You have just made Alison Engleman the happiest person in the world! Wait until I tell you my great idea!"

About the Author
Joan Lowery Nixon is the author of many books, and is especially well-known for her mysteries. This book came about from a desire to write "a funny mystery," one with a main character "who would be positive and energetic and interested in contemporary problems." Ms. Nixon lives in Houston, Texas.

Another of Ms. Nixon's books, *The House on Hackman's Hill*, is also available as an Apple paperback edition.

About the Illustrator
Amy Rowen has illustrated a number of books. She says this book was fun because "it is very *up*; the main characters are constantly moving, changing, doing new things. All that positive stuff rubs off!" Ms. Rowen lives in New York City.